the Cheetah Girls

Who's 'Bout to Bounce?

Deborah Gregory

D1019769

JUMP AT THE SUN

HYPERION PAPERBACKS FOR CHILDREN

NEW YORK

Fashion credits: Photography by Charlie Pizzarello. Models: Imani Parks, Mia Lee, Brandi Stewart, Arike Rice, and Jeni Rice-Genzuk. On Imani (Dorinda): leopard leotard by Jacques Moret Bodywear for Kids. On Arike (Aquanette): purple leopard top by to the max, black tie-front stretch capri pants by Essendi. On Jeni (Anginette): cheetah top by Daang Goodman for Tripp, NYC, black stretch capri pants by Malibu at The Vanity Room. All hosiery by Look From London. Hair by Jeffrey Woodley. Makeup by Lanier Long. Fashion styling by Sharon Chatmon Miller.

Printed in the United States of America.
First Edition
    5 7 9 10 8 6 4
This book is set in 12-point Palatino.
ISBN: 0-7868-1386-5
Library of Congress Catalog Card Number: 99-61155.

For my mother,
Ruth Gregory,
wherever you are

The Cheetah Girls Credo

To earn my spots and rightful place in the world, I solemnly swear to honor and uphold the Cheetah Girls oath:

- Cheetah Girls don't litter, they glitter. I will help my family, friends, and other Cheetah Girls whenever they need my love, support, or a *really* big hug.

- All Cheetah Girls are created equal, but we are not alike. We come in different sizes, shapes, and colors, and hail from different cultures. I will not judge others by the color of their spots, but by their character.

It is important to identify your significant other's desires and to take them into account in making decisions. In the long run, your relationship will be stronger if you give more consideration to both of your needs. The way you treat your partner will inevitably have a large impact on how you're treated in return. Set a high standard for caring and consideration and you'll both be happy.

17 to 23:
You've Found a Balance!

You have found the perfect balance of giving and receiving in your relationship. You manage to attend to your partner's needs while still taking care of yourself. You understand that relationships go more smoothly when both people look out for each other, as well as for themselves. You also recognize that compromising plays a critical role in any successful relationship. Congratulations on finding the right combination. Keep it up, and your relationship is sure to go the distance.

24 to 30:
You Make Sacrifices!

You have mastered a skill that is difficult for many people—putting the needs of others ahead of your own. While this ability is crucial for a deep relationship, it can present a problem when you forget about your own desires. You may need to work on balancing your tendency to be considerate with the importance of taking care of yourself. This can be difficult when you have strong feelings for someone and want to do everything you can to make that person happy. In the long run, you need to compromise so that you can both be happy, while maintaining a combination of mutual respect and consideration.

- A true Cheetah Girl doesn't spend more time doing her hair than her homework. Hair extensions may be career extensions, but talent and skills will pay my bills.

- True Cheetah Girls *can* achieve without a weave—or a wiggle, jiggle, or a giggle. I promise to rely (mostly) on my brains, heart, and courage to reach my cheetah-licious potential!

- A brave Cheetah Girl isn't afraid to admit when she's scared. I promise to get on my knees and summon the growl power of the Cheetah Girls who came before me—including my mom, grandmoms, and the Supremes—and ask them to help me be strong.

- All Cheetah Girls make mistakes. I promise to admit when I'm wrong and will work to make it right. I'll also say I'm sorry, even when I don't want to.

- Grown-ups are not always right, but they are bigger, older, and louder. I will treat my teachers, parents, and people of authority with respect—and expect them to do the same!

- True Cheetah Girls don't run with wolves or hang with hyenas. True Cheetahs pick much better friends. I will not try to get other people's approval by acting like a copycat.

- To become the Cheetah Girl that only *I* can be, I promise not to follow anyone else's dreams but my own. No matter how much I quiver, shake, shiver, and quake!

- Cheetah Girls were born for adventure. I promise to learn a language other than my own and travel around the world to meet my fellow Cheetah Girls.

Chapter 1

When you put the *C* to the *H* to the *A* to the *N* to the *E* to the *L*, you've got one supa-fast Cheetah *señorita*! I mean, Chanel "Chuchie" Simmons is all legs, even though she is only five feet two—which is just a little taller than me. All right, Chanel is *four* inches taller, but that's not the point.

Right about now, after jogging all the way from Soho, where Chanel lives, up to Harlem, where I live (which is more miles than the Road Runner does in one cartoon episode) the rest of us Cheetah Girls feel like wobbly cubs. We're desperate for a little shade and some soda!

Chanel, on the other hand, looks like *she's*

ready to do pirouettes or something. Now I can see why she used to take ballet lessons. She's got "gamma ray legs"!

"Wait up, Cheetah *Señorita*, yo!" I yell to Chanel, just to help her remember that she's not out here all by herself—that she is running with her crew. *Our* crew, that is. The Cheetah Girls.

Besides Chanel "Chuchie" Simmons, that would be:

Galleria "Bubbles" Garibaldi, who is the leader of our pack;

Aquanette and Anginette Walker, a.k.a. the "Huggy Bear twins"; and, of course, lucky me—Dorinda "Do' Re Mi" Rogers.

See, not too long ago, the five of us started a girl group, called the Cheetah Girls. You could pinch me every time I say it, 'cuz I still can't believe we got it like that.

Before I met my crew, I only sang for fun— you know, goofing around at home to entertain everybody. Bubbles and Chanel are the dopest friends I've ever had, and I'm so grateful that they got me to sing outside my bedroom.

I met them on our first day at Fashion Industries High School, where we are all freshmen, and it's the best thing that ever happened to me. Before, I was just plain old Dorinda Rogers. Now, I'm Do' Re Mi, which is the nickname my crew gave me. Do' Re Mi—one of the Cheetah Girls!

Bubbles and Chanel say we're gonna take over the world with our global groove. I hope they're right. For now though, we're just happy that Galleria's mom, Ms. Dorothea, has hooked us up with the famous Apollo Theatre Amateur Hour Contest! It's next Saturday—only a week and a half till we're up there, performing on that stage where the Supremes once sang. That is so *dope*!

See, Ms. Dorothea is not only Bubbles's mom—she has now officially become our manager. Our first manager was Mr. Jackal Johnson. We met him at the Cheetah-Rama Club, where we performed for the first time. He tried to manage us on the "okeydokey" tip. That means he was a crook.

When Ms. Dorothea found out Mr. Johnson was trying to get his hands on our duckets (not that we have any yet), she nearly threw him out the window! She doesn't play, you know what I'm sayin'?

Of course, Ms. Dorothea isn't out here

running with us today, because she is very busy with her boutique—Toto in New York . . . Fun in Diva Sizes—she runs the store, designs the clothes, and everything.

Aquanette says, "Dorothea's probably eating Godiva chocolates and laughing at us."

Word. She should talk! In fact, Aqua and Angie *both* like to eat a lot. If they keep it up, they're gonna be bigger than Dorothea by the time they're her age! (Dorothea used to be a model, but now she is "large and in charge," if you know what I mean!)

"Come on, Do' Re *Poor* Mi, move that matchstick butt!" heckles Chanel, poking out her tongue and "bugging" her eyes. Chanel is on a jelly roll, and she won't quit.

See, I can run almost as fast as her, but I don't wanna leave the rest of my crew behind.

I'm not flossin'. I can dance, skateboard, jump double Dutch, *and* I was the top tumbler in my gymnastics class last year in junior high, so what you know about that, huh?

Jackie Chan's got nothing on me, either. If I wanted to, I could do karate moves—well, if I had a black belt I could. At this point, I'd settle for a polka-dot belt, 'cuz you gotta watch your back in the jiggy jungle, especially in the part where I live, way up on 116th Street.

We've been running for a kazillion miles, and right about now Bubbles is at the end of her rope-a-dope.

"Chuchie, would you quit runnin' ahead of us? If you don't stop flossin', I'm gonna pull out one of your fake braids!" she snarls at the Cheetah *señorita*.

I start giggling. See, sometimes I'm scared to snap on Chanel or Bubbles, because I'm afraid if I do, then they won't let me be their friend.

Me, I'm just the new kid on the block. It's okay for them to snap on each other, though, 'cuz they've been friends forever—ever since Bubbles stole Chanel's Gerber Baby apple sauce—so they fight like sisters all the time.

They don't *look* like sisters, though. Bubbles is very light-skinned, and she has a really nice, full shape. About the only running she likes to do is to the dinner table, or to a party. I wish I had a shape like hers, instead of mine, which looks like a boy's.

Chanel is more tan and flat-chested, like me, and really skinny, too. But because she's taller, it looks really cute on her. She's kinda like a

Mexican jumping bean. She'll eat Chub Chub candies all day on the run, and keep jumpin'.

Anyhow, the reason why we're out here panting like puppies is not to lose weight. It's because Dorothea is putting us through this whole "divettes-in-training camp" thing, so we can become a legit girl group, like the Supremes or the Spice Rack Girls. That means we have to do what she says:

- We have to run five miles, at least once a week, to build up our endurance and lung power. This way, we'll be able to sing in big stadiums, and travel on the road without getting sore throats all the time.

- We have to take vocal lessons and dance classes.

- We have to watch old videos. Once a month, we have "Seventies Appreciation Night," which means we all get together over at Bubbles's house, and watch old videos of groups and movies with peeps in *mad* funny outfits.

- ❧ We have to develop other skills so we don't end up on the "chitlin' circuit." That's where singers go who don't even have a bucket to put their duckets in. They end up performing for no pay—they just pass a hat around for tips!

- ❧ We have to do our homework in school, read magazines, and dress dope, like divettes with duckets.

Chanel's mother, Juanita, has volunteered to run with us, but she is in better shape than we are and she just runs way ahead by herself. Since she's a grown-up, we don't mind. Because she is running ahead of us, she won't see us making faces, whining, giggling, and snapping on the peeps as we pass them by. Right now, though, we're too tired to even snap on a squirrel.

Juanita looks kinda funny from the back when she's running, because the bottom of her feet come up fast, like hooves on a horse, and her ponytail keeps bouncing up and down. She's kinda tall and skinny for a lady her age. See, she used to be a model, just like Dorothea (but *she* exercises like the Road Runner). Every now and then she looks back to ask us, "You girls all right?"

Poor Bubbles's mouth is hanging open, and she looks kinda mad, but she never gives up on anything. She just starts snapping. She sweats so much, though—there are droplets dripping down the side of her face, making her hair stick together like gooey sideburns!

The twins are kinda slow, too, but they don't complain a lot about running. Their minds are on other things.

"Do you really think the Sandman comes with a hook and pulls you off the stage if the audience boos you?" Anginette whines, running alongside me.

The Sandman at the Apollo Theatre is supposed to be this guy dressed like a scarecrow, with a big hook or something, who chases Amateur Hour contestants off the stage if they're wack.

"You sure he ain't like Jason from *Friday the 13th*?" Aquanette asks, chuckling nervously. Aqua and Angie are *Scream* queens. They love to watch horror movies with people getting their eyes poked out.

"I don't know, Angie," I say, panting, "but if the audience even *looks* like they're gonna start booing, then I'm gonna bounce, *before* the Sandman tries to hook us!"

"Oh, no, that is too wack-a-doodle-do! And it's not gonna happen," Bubbles says, smiling again. "We're gonna be in there like swimwear."

Galleria always makes us feel better. That's why she's Cheetah number one. Anything goes wrong, and we all look to her, just naturally. She's not takin' any shorts.

We are running in Central Park now, and suddenly, a funny-looking guy with a silver thing on his head zooms by on his bicycle, and almost runs down Aquanette. "Dag on, he almost knocked me over," yells Aqua, looking back at him as he rides away.

The twins are not used to the ways of the Big Apple, or how fast everybody moves here. They say everybody moves a lot slower in Houston, which is where they grew up—in a big house with a porch and everything in the suburbs.

"Beam me up, Scottie, you wack-a-doodle helmet head!" Galleria yells back at the guy on the bike, then gasps for breath. She sticks up for us a lot, because she isn't afraid of anybody.

"Y'all, there are a lot of crazy people here," Anginette chimes in.

"Helmet Head probably woulda knocked her over if nobody was looking!" Bubbles says.

"I wonder if that was a strainer on his head," Chanel says, giggling.

"And what were those funny-looking antenna things sticking up?" I giggle back.

"Come on, you lazy *muchachas*!" Juanita yells back at us, waving for us to follow her.

I don't know how long we've been running, but I am so grateful when we finally reach the park exit at 110th street.

"Thank *gooseness*," Galleria yelps, as we stop by the benches where Juanita is waiting for us impatiently, her hands on her hips. Bubbles bends over and is panting heavily, holding on to her knees. Her hair is so wild it's flopping all over the place like a mop.

This is where I get off, I think with a sad sigh. I wish I could invite my crew over to my house for some "Snapple and snaps." After all, I only live six blocks from here. But after seeing where *they* all live, I'm too embarrassed to let them see my home.

I live with my foster mother, Mrs. Bosco, her husband, Mr. Bosco, and about nine or ten foster brothers and sisters—depending on which day you ask me. We all share an apartment in the Cornwall Projects. We keep it clean, but still, it's real small and crowded. It needs some fixing up by the landlord, too—if you know what I'm sayin'.

It bothers me a lot to be a foster child but Mrs. Bosco is a pretty nice lady, even though she's not really my mom or anything—but now, I'm hanging with my new crew, and all of them have such nice houses, and real families. . . .

"Ms. Simmons, can't we at least *walk* to our house from here?" Angie asks, whining to Juanita.

Since I never invite anybody over, the next stop on this gravy train is the twins' house on 96th Street. Angie and Aqua live with their father in a nice apartment that faces Riverside Park. My apartment faces the stupid post office.

"Okay, lazy," Juanita huffs back.

"Well," I say, "bye, everybody."

Chanel puts her sweaty arms around me to kiss me good-bye.

"Ugh, Chanel!" I wince.

"Do' Re Mi, can't you see I love you!" she giggles back, kissing me on cheek and making silly noises. Then Chanel whispers in my ear, laying on the Spanish accent, "You know I was just playing *wichoo*. I know you can run as fast as me."

"Okay, *Señorita*, just get off me!" I giggle back. "Bye, Bubbles, and all you boo-boo heads!"

"Bye, Dorinda," Juanita says. Then she adds, "Don't stay up late, 'cuz *we're* going to bed *early*," giving me that look like "you better not be trying to hog the chat room on the Internet tonight."

See, Chanel's kinda grounded for life—until she pays back the money she charged on her mom's credit card last month. She's not supposed to be on the phone or the Internet, runnin' up more bills.

"See y'all tomorrow at school," I yell, then add, "not you two!" to Angie and Aqua. The twins don't go to Fashion Industries High, like me, Chanel, and Bubbles. They go to LaGuardia Performing Arts High School, which is even doper.

Maybe next year, me, Bubbles, and Chuchie can transfer to LaGuardia, so we can all be together. . . .

You know, you have to audition to get into LaGuardia. Chanel was too chicken to audition last year, coming out of junior high—even though Bubbles wanted to go to LaGuardia in the worst way. But Bubbles didn't want to audition without Chuchie, so they didn't go. That's why they both wound up at Fashion Industries, which is lucky for me!

But now, who knows? Sure, auditioning is kinda scary, but now that we're the Cheetah Girls, we've got each other, and we've had some experience performing—so I know we can do it.

Besides, Bubbles says if the Cheetah Girls really take off, and our lives get too hectic, we'll have to get private tutors anyway. Private tutors! Wouldn't that be the dopest?

That's Bubbles for you, always planning ahead to "destination: jiggy jungle." That's the place, she says, where dreams really do come true—*if* you go for *yours*.

Listening to Bubbles, we all feel like we really can do anything we set our minds to.

Chapter 2

I head uptown alone, on my way back to the apartment. Soon, my thoughts drift forward to next Saturday night.

What if the Sandman really does chase us off the stage? Or if somebody hits me on the head with a can of Burpy soda while I'm performing? Then I'll get a concussion . . . and I won't be able to take care of Mrs. Bosco and all my brothers and sisters. . . .

"Hey! Watch where you're goin', shorty!"

By the time I hear Can Man's warning, it's too late, 'cuz he's slammed his shopping cart filled with empty cans right into my back. I trip over a mound of rocks, and a thousand cans go flying everywhere.

"*You* watch where *you're* goin'!" I scream back at him. From my knees, I pick up a can and make like I'm gonna throw it at him.

Can Man is one of those people in New York who are out all day, collecting empty soda and beer cans, and returning them to places like the Piggly Wiggly supermarket around the corner for the deposit money.

In other words, he is a homeless man, but I think he is "sippin' more times than he is tip-pin'," because he screams a lot for no reason, and does wack things—like this.

"You better not take one of my cans, shorty!" Can Man yells. Now he is foaming at the mouth. His eyes are buggin', too.

I drop the can and run. I don't even listen to the people who ask me if they can help. No, they *can't* help me!

Why does everything happen to me? My real mother gave me away. My first foster mother, Mrs. Parkay, gave me up when I was little, for no reason. And now, Can Man runs into me with his stupid shopping cart!

My ankle really hurts, and I sit down on somebody's front stoop to massage it.

Sometimes I get scared that I'm just gonna

end up like a bag lady, and get married to Can Man or something. Who am I kidding? Maybe I'll never be anything! In fact, if it wasn't for my crew, I'd be just a wanna-be, I tell myself. Look at Bubbles and Chanel. You can tell they are born stars.

Me? Well, everybody says I can dance really good, and I guess I can sing okay. But I'm never gonna be famous. In fact, when I'm alone, and not with the group, I'm really scared of performing—and especially auditioning.

Now my legs *really* hurt from running all those miles, and I think Can Man might've broken my left ankle! I'm so mad, I wanna punch somebody. Let somebody—*anybody*—be stupid enough to get in my way now! Fuming like a fire engine, I hobble, step by step on my one good foot, to my apartment building.

"Hi, Dorinda! How come you limping?" asks Pookie, who is sitting in the courtyard. See, there are a lot of buildings in the Cornwall Projects, but only two of them have a courtyard, so all the kids hang out here.

Pookie is sitting with his mom, Ms. Keisha, and his sister, Walkie-talkie Tamela. We call her that because she never shuts up.

"Heh, Pookie," I respond, huffing and puffing. "Can Man hit me with his cart and knocked me over."

"You know he's crazy. You better stay out of his way, Dorinda, before he really hurts you," mumbles Ms. Keisha.

"I know, Ms. Keisha, but I didn't see him because he was behind me. Is Mrs. Bosco home?"

"Yep," she says, nodding her head at me. See, Ms. Keisha is nosy, and she knows that *we* know she's nosy. She sits outside all day, with a head full of pink hair rollers and even pinker bedroom slippers, talking about people's business like she's Miss Clucky on the gossip show.

Not that her motormouth doesn't come in "handy dandy," as Bubbles would say. See, if you're in trouble, and you wanna know if you're gonna get it when you get upstairs, you just ask Ms. Keisha. She knows if your mother is home—*and* if she's mad at you.

The courtyard isn't much of a playground for all the kids who live here, but it's better than hanging out in front with the "good-for-nothings," as Mrs. Bosco calls the knuckleheads who hang around all day and don't go to school or to work.

Some of the people who live here try to make it look nice, too. Once somebody tried to plant a tree right in the cement, but it was gone the next morning. So now there are no trees—just a few po' little brown shrubs that look like nubs. And there aren't any slides, swings, or jungle gym to play on, either—just some big old "X" marks scribbled with chalk on the ground, for playing jumping jacks.

I used to jump double Dutch rope out here all the time when I was little. I was the rope-a-dopest double Dutcher, too, even though Tawanna, who lives in Building C, thinks *she's* the bomb. She's such a big show-off, it just looks like she's got more moves than she *really* does.

It's getting dark out already. I know I've missed dinner, but Mrs. Bosco will still have something waiting for me. Hobbling on my good ankle, I open the door to the building, and get my keys out of my sweatpants. After dinner, I think, I'd better go see if Mrs. Gallstone down the hall is home. She's a nurse, and she'll know if my ankle is broken or not.

I hope little Arba is over her cold, too, I think, as I limp to the elevator. Arba is my new little sister. She's almost five years old—the same age I was when I came to live with Mrs. Bosco. She doesn't speak English very well, but we're teaching her.

Arba is Albanian by nationality, but her mother had her here, then died. Mrs. Bosco says a lot of people come to the Big Apple looking for the streets paved in gold, but instead they get "chewed up and spit out."

Most of the time, the caseworkers never say much about where foster kids come from, or what happened to them. They just drop them off, sometimes with bags of clothes and toys. Anyway, someone took Arba to the Child Welfare Department because she had no family, and they gave her to Mrs. Bosco to take care of until somebody adopts her—if anybody ever does.

You could say our house is kinda like the United Nations or something. My seven-year-old foster brother, Topwe, is African—real African, from Africa. He speaks English all funny, but it's his native language. They all talk like that over there!

Topwe gets the most attention, because he is

HIV-positive, which means he was infected with the AIDS virus. His mother was a crack addict, Mrs. Bosco told me, but I'm not supposed to say anything to Topwe or the other kids. I'm the only one, she says, who can keep a secret. It's true, too. I really can.

Like I said, the United Nations. There's Arba for one, and Topwe for another. Then there's my four-year-old brother, Corky, who is part Mexican and part Bajin. (Bajin is what you call people from Barbados, which is in the British West Indies.)

Corky is really cute, and he has the most beautiful greenish-gray eyes you've ever seen. His father is fighting with Child Welfare, trying to get him back. I hope he doesn't. I don't want Corky to leave.

I know kids are supposed to live with their families, but I feel like Corky's *my* family, too— I mean, he's been here practically his whole life! What's his father know about him, anyway?

See, sometimes the kids in our house go back to their real parents. Once in a blue moon, they even get adopted by new families, who are looking for a child to love. Nobody has ever tried to adopt *me*, though.

Sometimes I cry about that—nobody wanting me. See, most parents who adopt want little kids, and by the time I got to Mrs. Bosco's, I was already too old—almost five. So yeah, it hurts when one of my brothers or sisters gets adopted and I don't. But I feel glad to have a place to live anyway. It could be worse—I could be out on the street, like a lot of other people. Like Can Man . . .

Besides, we may not have much, but life is pretty good here. We all stick up for each other when the chips are down. And Mrs. Bosco loves us all—she just doesn't let herself show it very often. I guess it's because that way, it won't hurt so much when the caseworkers take one of her kids away.

Even in the lobby, I can tell that somebody upstairs is cooking fried chicken. I *love* fried chicken—with collard greens, potato salad, and corn bread. That's the bomb meal.

We call where we live the "Corn Bread Projects" since, when you walk down the hallway, you can smell all the different kinds of food people are cooking in their apartments.

That's actually better than the elevators, which sometimes smell like *eau de pee pee*.

When the elevator door closes now, I get a whiff of some nasty smell. I hold my breath the whole ride up.

Everybody says the Cornwall Projects are dangerous, but nobody bothers us around here. That's because my foster father, Mr. Bosco, is *really* big, and he wears a uniform to work—plus he has a nightstick he says is for "clubbing knuckleheads."

He is a security guard who works the night shift, so he sleeps during the day. Most of us kids don't see him much, but he is really nice. He laughs like a big grizzly bear. Both times I got skipped in school, he gave me five dollars and said, "I'll give you five dollars every time you get skipped again!"

Chapter 3

As soon as I open the front door of the apartment, Twinkie jumps out from the corner. That's the game we play every day.

"Hey, Twinkie!" I say to my favorite sister, who is nine years old. Her real name is Rita, but we call her Twinkie, because she has blond fuzzy hair, and fat, yummy cheeks.

"Don't call me Twinkie anymore!" she announces to me, shuffling the deck of Pokémon cards she has in her hands. Twinkie grabs my hand, and pulls me down the hallway to the kitchen. Everybody else has eaten already, but Mrs. Bosco always puts my food in the oven, covered in a piece of tinfoil. All the kids know they'd better not touch it, either.

"I have to whisper something in your ear," Twinkie says, pulling me down so she can reach.

"Okay," I say, hugging her real tight. Twinkie has lived with us for nineteen months, and we are really close—she will always be my sister forever, no matter what.

"You have to call me Butterfly now," Twinkie tells me, and her blue eyes get very big, like saucers.

"Okay, Cheetah Rita Butterfly!" I giggle, then tickle her stomach, which I know sends her into hysterics.

"Stop!" she screams. "You big Cheetah monkey!"

"What's a Cheetah monkey, Cheetah Rita Butterfly?" I ask, poking her stomach some more. "Tell me, tell me, or I'm not gonna stop!"

"I don't know, but *you* are!" she screams, and giggles even more hysterically.

"Okay, I'll call you Cheetah Rita Butterfly, if you promise that we are gonna be sisters forever. You're never gonna get away from me!"

"Okay, okay!" she screeches, and I stop tickling her. After a minute, she stops laughing. "We're not really sisters though, are we?"

Twinkie asks me with that cute little face.

"Yes, we are," I say.

"Then how come we have different last names?" Twinkie asks, suddenly all serious. She is so smart.

"That doesn't mean we're not sisters, Cheetah Rita."

"Okay, then, I promise," Twinkie says, teasing me, then she runs off, daring me to chase her. "I'm Cheetah Rita Butterfly! Watch me fly so high!"

Putting one of the Pokémon cards from the jungle deck over one eye, Twinkie turns, then squinches up her face and yells, "Dorinda!"

"What?" I turn to answer her back.

"You can call me Twinkie again!" She giggles up a storm as I chase her down the hallway into her room, yelling, "You little troublemaker!"

Twinkie shares her bedroom with Arba, who I already told you about, and my sister Kenya.

Kenya is six, and she is a "special needs child," because she is always getting into trouble at school, or fighting with the other kids. But I don't think she is "emotionally disturbed" like they say. She is just selfish, and doesn't like to share anything, or listen to anybody. Twinkie and Arba don't seem to like sharing a room with Kenya. Can't say I blame them.

I share a bedroom—a tiny one—with my two *other* sisters, Chantelle and "Monie the Meanie." Monie is the oldest out of all of us. She is seventeen, and has a major attitude problem. I'm so glad she has a boyfriend now—Hector—and she's over at his house a lot. She doesn't like to help clean or anything, and she likes to boss me around. I wish she would just go stay with Hector. It would make more room for me and Chantelle.

Chantelle is eleven, but tries to act like she's grown already, sitting around reading *Sistarella* magazine, and hogging my computer.

Mr. Hammer gave *me* the computer last year. He's our super, and he knows how to fix everything—and who throws out what. He told me that a tenant from one of the other buildings was gonna throw out her computer, and he got her to give it to me. I call Mr. Hammer "Inspector Gadget," 'cuz he's got the hookup, if you know what I'm saying.

The boys all share the biggest bedroom. That would be Topwe and Corky, along with Khalil (who has only lived here two months), Nestor (who we nicknamed Nestlé's Quik because he eats really fast), and "Shawn the Fawn" (we call him that because he's really shy, and always runs away from people). Four of the boys sleep in bunk beds to make more space.

Mr. and Mrs. Bosco's bedroom used to be the pantry—that's how small it is. But since Mrs. Bosco is up all day with us kids, and Mr. Bosco works all night, usually only one of them sleeps at a time—so I guess it doesn't seem as small to them as it does to us.

Every time one of us leaves for good, I always think the Boscos will switch bedrooms around. But they never do. They always go and get another foster child to fill the empty bed. That's the way they are. Lucky for all of us . . .

I have followed Twinkie into her bedroom. Arba is sitting there on the floor, drawing with crayons, and Kenya has her mouth poked out, staring at a page in her school notebook. She's always mad about something. I feel bad for her. But I know if I ignore her, then she will at least act nice for five minutes, trying to get my attention.

I pretend Kenya isn't even there. "There's Arba!" I exclaim, kissing her dirty face. Then I sit on the floor to take off my smelly sneakers and socks.

That gets Kenya. "Abba!" she yells, taking a crayon from Arba's hand. Kenya never pronounces anybody's name right. "Don't eat that!"

"She wasn't gonna eat it, Kenya," I say, forgetting that I'm trying to ignore her.

Kenya sticks out her tongue at me, happy to have gotten my attention.

"Abba-cadabra," chants Twinkie, suddenly taking off her shorts. "I'm smelly. I'm gonna take my bath first, okay?"

"I'm smelly, too." I giggle. "You feel better, Arba?"

"Bubba bath! Bubba bath!" she says, smiling.

Then I hear Mrs. Bosco coughing in the living room. "You take your bath first, Twinkie," I say. "I'll be right back."

Mrs. Bosco just got out of the hospital last week. She was real sick, and she still has to rest a lot. When I go in the living room, I see her lying on the plastic-covered couch, with a blanket pulled over her. The lights are off in here, so that's why I didn't see her when I first came in.

"Hi, Mrs. Bosco. What's the matter?" I ask

her. She doesn't really like to kiss or hug much, and she says I don't have to call her Mom. I guess that's good, because I called my last foster mother Mom, and she gave me away. Still, I sure wish I had *somebody* I could call Mom.

"My arthritis is acting up again." Mrs. Bosco moans.

"Lemme rub your arms," I tell her. She likes when I give her massages, and I think it helps her arthritis too.

"No, baby—or . . . what your friends call you now?"

"Do' Re Mi," I tell her with a giggle.

"That's right. You go and get your Do' Re Mi self some dinner. I'll be awright," Mrs. Bosco says, chuckling and waving her hand.

Then she gets serious. "Oh, Dorinda— Kenya's teacher called today, and said she's having trouble with that child. Seems she's stealing things from the other kids. Can you talk to her? She'll listen to you."

"Okay," I yell back.

"And when you get a chance, look at that letter from the electric company. I don't have my glasses on. Tell me what it says." Mrs. Bosco sighs, and lies down again.

Mrs. Bosco can't read or write. We're not supposed to know this, but I don't mind taking care of the bills for her, because if the social workers find out, she won't be able to have any more foster kids.

"Is something wrong with your leg?" Mrs. Bosco asks me as I hobble to the kitchen.

"Yeah, I think my ankle is broken," I whine.

"If it was broken, you wouldn't be able to walk on it, but you'd better let Mrs. Gallstone look at it. Oh, I almost forgot. What's the name of that lady where you take them classes?"

"You mean Drinka Champagne?"

"No, I remember her. You know, I was young once, too—'tippin' and sippin',' like her song says. No, I mean the other lady you talk about—at the YMCA."

"Oh, Ms. Darlene Truly?" I ask, squinching up my nose.

"What's that child's name?" is another "game" we play, because Mrs. Bosco can't write down the messages, so she tries to remember who called, and sometimes she forgets.

"Yeah, that's her. She said it's very important for you to call her if you ain't coming to class tomorrow, because she needs to talk to you—

and it's very important," Mrs. Bosco repeats herself. Then she adds, rubbing her forehead, "Lord, now I got a headache, too."

I want to tell Mrs. Bosco to take off her wig, and maybe that would help her headache, but Mrs. Bosco doesn't take off her wigs until she goes to bed at night. She is wearing this new one that we ordered from It's a Wig!, but it looks terrible. It's kinda like the color silver gets when it's rusted, even though the color was listed as "salt and pepper" in the catalogue.

Why is Ms. Truly calling me? I wonder. I can feel a knot in my stomach. She's never called me at home before, and I don't like people bothering Mrs. Bosco. I must have done something wrong!

"I don't know what Ms. Truly wants," I say, "but I'll probably see her before class, since I'm working at the YMCA concession stand after school tomorrow."

I don't want Mrs. Bosco to worry about anything, or think I'm in trouble for some reason. She has enough to worry about.

"How'd you hurt your leg, Dorinda?"

"I fell," I say. "Can Man hit me with his cart.

Maybe it was my fault, anyway. I'm just gonna put ice on it and go to bed."

Luckily, Mrs. Gallstone said my ankle isn't broken. It's just strained. I hate going over to her apartment, because the kitty litter box really stinks. I made it a really quick visit, telling her I had to get back home and go to bed early.

It's only nine o'clock, but it's been a long, hard day. Once I lie down on my bed, I'm too tired to get up and put ice on my ankle after all. Chantelle is popping her gum so loud—but if I say anything, she'll get an attitude, so I just ignore her.

On a table in between her bed and mine is my Singer sewing machine. I'm trying to design a new costume for the Cheetah Girls, but I haven't figured out what to do on the bodice.

Oh, well. I'm too tired to work on it tonight. Instead, I turn my face to the wall. I'm even too beat to take off my shorts and take a shower!

As usual, whenever I'm lying awake in bed, things start bothering me.

What if I'm really not a good singer after all? If

the Cheetah Girls find out, then they are gonna kick me out of the group. They probably only let me stay in the group because they feel sorry for me, anyway.

"How come you wuz limping?" Chantelle asks me, popping her gum extra loud.

"Can Man hit me from behind with his shopping cart," I moan, hoping Chantelle will stop bothering me.

What does Ms. Truly want? I wonder. Please tell me, crystal ball. I wish I knew a psychic like Princess Pamela—she's Chanel's father's girlfriend, and she can read the future. But I'm not close enough to her to get her to read mine for free, and I don't have any money to pay her.

I get real quiet, thinking again. I'll bet Ms. Truly doesn't want me to take dance classes anymore, because there are other kids who need them more than I do. Or maybe the YMCA found out that I'm not really fourteen! That's it—they're gonna kick me out of the Junior Youth Entrepreneurship Program!

I know if I keep this up, I'll be awake all night. So I make myself go to sleep by thinking about my favorite dream. In my dream, I am dancing across the sky, and I see my real mother in the clouds, smiling at me. I can dance so high that she starts clapping.

Dozing off, I whisper to myself so that Chantelle doesn't hear me, "Dancing in the clouds, that's me—I'm not just another wanna-be. . . ."

Chapter 4

Two days a week after school, I work the concession stand at the YMCA on 135th Street as part of the Junior Youth Entrepreneurship Program, which teaches peeps like me skills to pay the bills—marketing, salesmanship, motivational training, and stuff like that.

It's almost six o'clock, and I'm kinda nervous because I haven't seen Ms. Truly walk by yet. She teaches a dance class here—earlier than the one I take—so I thought I would see her going to the cafeteria for a soda or something between classes. Sucking my teeth, I realize I must have missed her, because I was too busy folding these boring T-shirts!

Abiola Adams works the stand with me.

Who's 'Bout to Bounce?

She's a freshman at Stuyvesant High School, and studies ballet at the American Ballet Theater School in Lincoln Center. In other words, she's smart *and* she's got mad moves.

I call her "Miss Nutcracker"—and she's really cool, 'cuz she's into flava like me. She has on this dope vest with red embroidery like paisley flowers, and baggy jeans. We are both wearing the same black Madd Monster stomp shoes.

"You know why nobody is buying these T-shirts?" I turn to Abiola with a mischievous smile on my face.

Abiola is sitting like a high priestess of price tags on a high chair, tagging baseball caps stamped with the YMCA moniker in big, ugly white letters. "Why?" she says, trying to stuff a yawn.

"'Cuz they're having a wack attack, that's why," I say with a frown. "See, if they would let me design the shirts, they'd be flying off the rack."

"Well then, why don't you ask them if you can? You could put, 'Cheetah Girl is in the house at the YMCA, yo!'" Abi says sarcastically.

"I'm not trying to floss. I'm serious, Abba-cadabra," I say, smiling, 'cuz I'm imitating my sister Twinkie. "This lettering could put a hurtin' on a blind man's eyesight. Who's gonna pay fifteen dollars for these T-shirts, anyway, when they can go to Chirpy Cheapies and get one for $5, with their *own* name stamped on it?"

"They don't charge extra for that?" Abiola asks me, like she's a news reporter or something.

"I don't know, but you know what I'm sayin'. I'm not playin'. Next semester, I get to take an embossing class, so I'll learn how to do some dope lettering. You watch."

"I will," Abiola says, shaking her head at me. What I like best about her is she can keep a secret. See, she's the only one here at the YMCA program who knows that I'm only twelve.

Sometimes I feel bad because I haven't even told my crew yet—but I don't want them treating me like a baby or something. I didn't mean to tell Abiola, but it just kinda slipped out one day.

See, she was telling me about the trick candles her mother put on her birthday cake. No matter how hard she blew, they wouldn't blow out. So I slipped, and told her how on my last birthday, Mrs. Bosco only put eleven candles on my cake instead of twelve. I thought it was so funny that she forgot how old I was.

See, when I was in elementary school and junior high, I hated how all the kids used to make fun of me, just because I was in the "SP" programs—that means Special Program for kids who are smart. But Abiola is real cool—she won't say anything, because I could lose my spot in the Junior Youth Program.

Okay, so you're supposed to be fourteen to be in the program. But on the other hand, it's for high school students—and that's what I am, right?

"Guess where I hear they're hiring?" Abiola says, all confidential like a secret agent.

"Where?" I ask, my eyes opening wide like flying saucers.

"At the Project Wise program at University Settlement, down on Eldridge Street on the Lower East Side," she whispers.

"Word?"

"Mmm-hmm. I hear they're paying the same as here—minimum wage, two nights a week. But in the summer, you can put in twenty-four

hours a week, and they got all kinds of programs."

"Yeah?"

"Uh-huh. They got this dope dance program,
I hear," Abiola says, nodding her head, then
turning to see if anyone is looking. "You sit
around and tell stories about your culture, then
you interpret it into dance, and at the end of the
year, you put on a big show called the Roots
Celebration."

"Word? You think I could go down there?" I
ask aloud.

"Try. They may not ask for your birth certificate or anything—just a letter from one of your
teachers at school, so they won't know you're
only twelve."

"Shhh," I smirk, putting my finger over my
mouth.

"Nobody heard me," Abiola says, giggling,
then putting some more of the ugly T-shirts in
a stack on the concession stand.

"Look at the new leotard I got," I say, pulling
my cheetah all-in-one out of my backpack to
show to Abiola. "Mrs. Bosco bought it for me
out of the money I gave her from the Cheetah
Girls show at the Cheetah-Rama on Halloween.

Four hundred duckets! I couldn't believe it. But I didn't keep the loot, because I knew Mrs. Bosco needed the money for her hospital bills."

"She sick?"

"Uh-huh. She coughs all the time."

"Where'd she find a cheetah leotard like that?" Abiola asks, smiling. She thinks it's cute that I'm a Cheetah Girl now.

"I think at Daffy's, or Chirpy's," I say, then let out a sigh. "I wonder why Ms. Truly wants to see me."

"Don't know, but you'll find out soon enough, 'cuz it's time to go with the flow," Abiola says, then grabs her bag to leave. She goes upstairs to the computer room, to work on the youth program's newsletter, *Mad Flava*.

Sometimes Abiola acts like she's a newscaster or something, like Starbaby Belle on television—but she's learning mad skills. So I guess she's got a right to floss a little.

The butterflies in my stomach start flapping their wings again as I change into my leotard. Then they flap some more when I walk into the gymnasium where I take Ms. Truly's hip-hop dance class.

That's the only thing I really like about working here—taking free dance classes. And now I may even lose that? It's not fair!

Pouting, I think of something Mrs. Bosco always says. "You can get mad, till you get glad!" It makes me laugh. She used to always say it to Jimmy, one of my used-to-be foster brothers. He used to walk around with his lips poked out so far, you'd think someone had stuffed them with platters. Then one day, his real mother decided she wanted him back, so they came and took him away from us. I haven't seen or heard from him since.

I wonder where Jimmy is now? I'm gonna ask my caseworker, Mrs. Tattle, when I see her. That's *if* I see her. Lately, the caseworkers have been coming and going, quittin' their jobs so fast it could make your head spin. Mrs. Bosco says, "For the little money they get paid, it's a miracle they show up at all."

"Dorinda! There you are. Why didn't you return my phone call?" Ms. Truly asks me sternly, as I take my place on the gym floor. She doesn't smile much, and it makes me kinda nervous.

"I thought you said to call you if I *wasn't* coming to class," I say, getting nervous again.

"No. I spoke to your mother, and I distinctly told her to have you call me *before* you came to class today," Ms. Truly insists.

"Oh, I'm sorry, Ms. Truly. Sometimes Mrs. Bosco, um, writes down the messages wrong because she's so busy," I say, trying to cover up for my foster mother. I wish Mrs. Bosco could read and write, but she never finished school.

"Well, that's all right, but don't leave without seeing me after class," Ms. Truly says.

I *hate* when grown-ups do that. Why don't they just blurt out whatever it is they want to say, and get it over with!

Usually, I stay near the front of the class, but today I'm so nervous that I go to the back, where Paprika is standing. Maybe *she* knows something, because she is one of Ms. Truly's "pets."

Ms. Truly always starts the class with warm-up *pliés*. So while we're doing them, going up and down, up and down, I turn to Paprika and whisper, "Did Ms. Truly talk to you about anything?"

"No, why?" Paprika asks, extending her arms out in second position.

"'Cuz she called my house and said she

wanted to see me after class today," I say nervously. I'm sweating already, and we haven't even started dancing yet.

"I don't know anything," Paprika says, giving me this serious look, like, "You must be in trouble, so get away from me!"

Bending my body over my feet, I feel like a croaked Cheetah.

Some hyena is coming in for the kill. I can *feel* it.

Usually, class is over much too soon, but today, I thought it would go on and on till the break of dawn! I guess that's good, though, since this will probably be the last class I take with Ms. Truly.

Sighing out loud, I pick up my towel and walk to the front of the gymnasium to wait for her. She's not even finished talking to the other students, before I start apologizing again for not calling her back.

"That's all right, Dorinda," Ms. Truly says sternly, "it's just that you won't have much time to practice."

"Practice?" I say, squinching up my nose because now I'm really confused. "Practice for what?"

"Come inside my office for a second," Ms. Truly says, taking me by my arm and leading me outside the gym to her office.

I can feel my heart pounding right through my cheetah leotard. I think it's gonna pop out of my chest like in *Alien* and start doing pirouettes or something!

Ms. Truly's perfume is strong. I know this smell. It's Fetch by Ruff Lauren, the perfume Bubbles likes.

"Sit down," Ms. Truly says, then closes the door.

I flop down in the chair like I have spaghetti legs. I must *really* be in trouble, 'cuz Ms. Truly is being super-nice to me. That's not like her.

Suddenly, a lightbulb goes off in my dim head. Ms. Truly probably wants to hook me up with an audition at *another* school or something, so she can get *rid* of me! I am getting so upset, I have to fight back the tears.

Ms. Truly pulls out a folder, looks at a piece of paper, then mutters, "There's still time. Can you stay after class tonight?"

"Yes." I croak like a frog, because the word got stuck somewhere down my throat. I wish Bubbles were here. She'd stand up and fight for me. So what you know about that, Ms. Truly? What a phony-baloney. Always acting like she likes me, but she doesn't!

"Okay," Ms. Truly says. Then she sighs, like she's Judge Fudge on television and she's gonna read me the verdict for a death penalty or something. "A friend of mine just got hired as the choreographer for the upcoming Mo' Money Monique tour, 'The Toyz Is Mine.' It's a one-year tour around the world, and they're looking for backup dancers, with hip-hop and some jazz training." She gives me a look. "I think you should audition for it."

All of a sudden, I feel like the scarecrow in *The Wizard of Oz* when he got cut down off his post. I just wanna flop to the floor in relief. *Ms. Truly thinks I can audition for Mo' Money Monique!*

"The only thing is, the audition is tomorrow morning. But if you stay after class tonight, we can practice for about half an hour. That way you'll go in there with full confidence, and be able to work your magic," Ms. Truly says, all smiley-faced.

I am so stunned, I must be acting like a zombie, because Ms. Truly looks at me and says,

"Dorinda, are you with me?"

"Yes, Ms. Truly. I'll, um, stay after class and go to the audition," I say, stuttering with excitement.

"Here, take the name of my friend, and the address where you have to go for the audition." Ms. Truly hands me a piece of paper.

"Dorka Por-i-," I read, but I'm having trouble pronouncing the lady's last name.

Ms. Truly helps me. "Por-i-skova," she says with a smile.

"Poriskova," I say, this time pronouncing it correctly. "What kind of name is that?"

"It's Czech."

"Oh," I say.

"The Czech Republic is a country in eastern Europe," Ms. Truly says.

"I know that," I tell her. I do, too. Geography is one of my best subjects in school. "It's near Albania, where my new sister Arba is from."

"I'm impressed!" Ms. Truly beams at me. "Anyway, you're gonna like Dorka. She's a fierce choreographer, and she's got 'mad moves,' as you would say. We studied at Joffrey Ballet together, back in the day."

"I didn't know you took ballet, Ms. Truly!" I

say, getting more excited. "My best friend, Chanel, used to take ballet. It's really hard, right?"

"Sure is," she agrees. "I wouldn't trade anything now for hip-hop, though. It gives you the cultural freedom to express yourself—and that's more important than any perfect *plee-ay*," she says, stretching out the word.

"I always had this secret fantasy about being a ballerina," I confide in Ms. Truly. "I wish I could have taken classes when I was little."

"Well, that's what daydreams are for," Ms. Truly says, chuckling like she knows. "You've got a feel for hip-hop though, Dorinda, and if you stick with it, you'll probably be able to write your own ticket."

I'm not sure what kind of ticket Ms. Truly is talking about, and I'm afraid to tell her how much I like being a Cheetah Girl. I don't want her to think I'm not grateful for the chance to audition for the Mo' Money Monique tour.

As if reading my mind, Ms. Truly says, "You're thinking about that group of yours, aren't you? I see you girls together all the time. It must be very exciting for you."

"Yes, Ms. Truly," I admit.

She sighs, gives me a sad smile. "I tried to be a singer once," she says. "But it just wasn't happening. I couldn't play the games you have to play to get a record deal."

She gives me a big smile now. "You'll have more control over your career as a dancer, Dorinda. The worst that could happen is, you'll end up a teacher, like me—and that's not so bad, is it?"

"No, Ms. Truly. You're the *best* teacher. You're dope," I say, hoping I haven't hurt her feelings.

"And you're the best dancer, Dorinda. It's a joy to teach you," Ms. Truly says, then comes around the desk to put her arms around me. Her hug makes me feel like a grilled shrimp, because she is so tall. *Everybody* is taller than me.

"I just hope one day you'll know what a great dancer you are," she says.

I can barely believe it's true—that Ms. Truly thinks I'm such a great dancer. But what about the Cheetah Girls? How can I leave them and my family, and go off around the world for a whole year?

All of a sudden, I feel like a total crybaby. I'm so exhausted from being nervous, I just let the tears come, one by one.

Ms. Truly holds me, and whispers, "Just give it all you've got tomorrow at the audition. God will take care of the rest." She lifts my chin in her hand and gives me a wink. "And make sure to wear this leotard," she adds. "It's *fierce.*"

Chapter 5

I smile all the way home, thinking about Ms. Truly and my audition. That is, until I have to hold the stupid ice pack on my ankle for a whole hour so that the swelling will go down. I shouldn't have taken class, I tell myself.

But how was I to know it wasn't going to be my last class? How was I supposed to know there was a big audition in my future? What do I have, a crystal ball?

I ask God to please make the swelling go down tomorrow for my big audition. I also wonder if God could get Chantelle to stop popping her gum like a moo-moo.

Since I'm too nervous to go to sleep, I hobble quietly into the kitchen to call Bubbles's and

Chanel's pagers. When one of us wants to talk in the chat room on the Internet, but it's too late to talk on the phone, we page each other. Whoever gets the page first is supposed to call Angie and Aqua, then all five of us assemble in the chat room. I wish I had a telephone in my room, but then Monie would probably hog it anyway, talking to her knucklehead boyfriend.

When I was little, she used to wake me up when I was sleeping, because she said I snored. That was before I got my tonsils out, but I don't think I really snored. She just hated me because, even then, I was Mrs. Bosco's favorite.

As I log on to the Internet, it hits me—*I can't tell my crew about the audition!* That really makes me feel like a Wonder Bread heel. What was I thinking, agreeing to audition as a backup dancer, when I'm already a part of a superhot group?

Well, it's too late now. I already said I'd go. Besides, it won't be the first secret I've kept from my crew. They still don't know how I live, really. Or how old I am.

Besides, I'm not gonna get this gig anyway. I don't care how good a dancer Ms. Truly thinks I am. I mean, we're talking about Mo' Money

Monique, you know what I'm saying? I bet Ms. Truly is sending a lot of girls to audition for the Dorky lady. I'll probably run into Paprika there.

As it turns out, I don't have to worry about telling my crew anything, because Bubbles needs to blab tonight. So I'm safe—for now.

"What makes you think your mom has hired some Bobo Baboso private detective?" Chanel types on the screen. That makes me laugh, 'cuz Chanel is making a snap on this television show on the Spanish channel, about a bumbling detective, Bobo Baboso, who fumbles cases.

"I'm telling you, my mom's hired a private detective, Miss Cuchifrito, so don't get 'chuchie' with me!" Bubbles types in.

"Why would she need to hire a private detective, Bubbles, can you tell us that?" Chuchie asks.

"NO! If I knew the answer to that, I wouldn't be asking all of you!" Bubbles is mad—she's reading Chanel.

"Why don't you just ask your mom what's going on—maybe she'll tell you," I type on the screen.

Then I feel sad, because I wish I could take my own advice and just be *honest*. Now that would *really* be dope.

My fingernails look like stub-a-nubs. I've bitten them off because I'm *mad* nervous. I'm so glad Bubbles isn't here, because she would be readin' me, but I couldn't help myself!

I feel *really* guilty that I didn't tell my crew last night about the audition, but I don't want them to think I'm not mad serious about being a Cheetah Girl. On the other hand, sometimes you gotta flex, you know what I'm saying?

Not that I'm flexing now. There are so many tall girls at the Mo' Money Monique audition that I feel like a grilled shrimp, as usual. I think maybe Ms. Truly made a mistake, because most of the girls here look older than me. *None* of them looks my age. My *real* age, you know what I'm saying?

I've got to chill. Maybe they'll never get to my number. After all, just by looking at these dancers' "penguin feet," I can tell they've got *mad* moves. They'll just send the rest of us home long before they get to my piddly place.

Who's 'Bout to Bounce?

I have never seen so many people waiting in line before. Not one, but *two* lines. Not even at the MC Rabbit concert last summer. Both lines are trailing like an out-of-control choo-choo train, all the way down the endless hallway outside of Rehearsal Studio A, where the audition is.

I'm so far back in line, I can't even hear what music they're playing inside the studio. I can only feel the vibration from the bass, thumping through the wall. They're probably using one of Mo' Money Monique's tracks. I really like her songs, so that's cool.

Right now, she has two of the dopiest dope hits out: "Don't Dis Me Like I'm a Doll" and "This Time It's Personal." They play them a kazillion times a day on the radio. I like the second one better, because it has more of the rap flava that I savor.

I wonder if I'm in the right line. . . . One line is for even numbers, and the other is for odd numbers. I'm number 357. Since I don't have any nails left to bite, I start yanking and twirling the curls on the side of my face. I'd better ask somebody if I'm on the right line, I think—just to make sure.

"What number are you?" I nervously ask the girl in front of me, who is wearing a red crop top and a baseball cap turned backward. I don't think she heard me, because she doesn't answer me, so I ask her again.

"Three hundred and *fifty-five*," she turns and snarls at me, giving me a nasty look, like, "I heard you the first time, shorty."

That's awright, Miss Pigeon. At least I'm not wearing wack contact lenses that make me look like the girl in *The Exorcist*!

"Girls, keep the aisles clear, please," yells a *really really* tall guy wearing a black leotard and tights. He is the one who wrote my name down and gave me a number, like we're in the bakery or something. All I can see of him now is the top of his really bald head, until he comes closer a few minutes later, with his clipboard in his hand like he's a high school principal.

"Everyone is going to get seen," says the exasperated giant, "and crowding the front, or hanging out in the middle of the hallway, isn't going to help the lines move any faster!"

All of a sudden, he adjusts his headset, then barks into it, "They're coming out? Okay, copy that. I'll send the next group in." Then he prances away like a gazelle. You can always tell a dancer, because they don't run like normal people. Except for me, 'cuz I don't floss like that.

Another hour goes by, which means I've been waiting in line for *two* hours now, and my throat is so dry it feels like it's gonna start croaking up frogs any minute.

I shoulda brought a Snapple and an apple, I chuckle to myself. But it's no joke, how sore my ankle is getting from standing around here so long. What if I can't dance because my ankle stiffens up or something?

The girl in front of me must be getting nervous too, because all of a sudden, she starts acting nice. "I need to stretch my legs," she says, sucking her teeth, then takes off her cap and pulls out a mirror to fix her hair. "I'm gonna be mad late for class. Do you think I should wear the cap, or keep it off?"

"I think you should keep it off—and maybe put your hair up, or something," I advise Miss Pigeon. She's dark brown, like Aqua and Angie, and her long blond extensions are so thick and straight, it looks like somebody played pin the donkey on her head. I think she should take off her big gold earrings, too, but I'm not gonna tell her that.

"You know how many dancers they're gonna pick?" Miss Pigeon asks me, pulling down her red crop top.

"No, but it must be a lot, 'cuz they're seeing a lot of dancers," I say, trying to act like I know something.

"No, I don't think Mo' Money Monique likes a lot of dancers onstage with her. It wrecks her flow. I bet you they're gonna pick about five—at the most," Miss Pigeon says, looking at me with those scary green *Exorcist* eyes.

"Where do you, um, go to school?" I ask, trying to be nice back. She must be a senior, I'm guessing.

"LaGuardia," she says nonchalantly. Folding her arms in front of her, she leans on the wall, like she is *really* bored.

I get so excited, I almost tell her that part of my crew goes to LaGuardia too. Then I realize—*What if she knows Aqua and Angie?* Then she'll tell them she met me at an audition for backup dancers!

Probably everybody at LaGuardia knows Aqua and Angie because they're twins—who can sing. I get so scared thinking about what I almost just did, I don't even hear Miss Pigeon asking me a question.

"I'm sorry, what'choo say?"

"Where do *you* go to school?"

For a second, I think about lying, but then I'll be frying, so I decide to tell the truth. "Fashion Industries."

"Oh," she says, like I don't have skills.

I am so grateful when the not-so-jolly giant calls our numbers, so I don't have to talk anymore to Miss Pigeon. My own thoughts come flooding back at me—mainly, "How could you go on an audition without telling your crew?"

"Okay, you girls can go inside now," Mr. Giant with the clipboard says, pointing to five girls, including me and Miss Pigeon. This is it—time to do or die.

When I get inside, I nervously look around and see one, two, *five* people sitting at a long table with a pitcher of water on it and some paper cups. I'd audition with that pitcher on my head, just to get a sip of what's inside!

I don't see Mo' Money Monique anywhere. At least I won't make a fool of myself in front of her.

A tall lady with a long ponytail and a bump on her nose motions for us to stand in a single line in front of her. She is really pretty, and I can tell that she used to be a ballerina, just by the way she is standing.

"Hell-o, lade-eez, I'm Dorka Poriskova, the choreographer. First I want you to introduce yourselves one by one, then I'll give you the combee-nay-shuns for the dance sequence to follow."

"I'm Dorinda Rogers," I say, speaking up loudly when it's my turn. Dorka has a really heavy accent, and I want to make sure she understands me.

"A-h-h," says Dorka with a smile. "We have the same name."

"I said *Dorinda Rogers*," I repeat, louder, 'cuz she obviously didn't understand me the first time.

"I know what you *said*, Dor-een-da," Dorka says, stretching my name out.

Omigosh! Now I've made her mad at me! Why did I have to open my big fat trap—my *boca grande*, as Chanel would say. I'm finished even before I get started!

"Each of our names means 'God's gift,'"

Dorka explains patiently. "Yours is the Spanish, um, var-ee-ay-shun, and mine is Czech."

"Oh," I say with a smile, but I'm so embarrassed, I want to shrivel right down to the size of a pebble and roll away! I act like I'm so smart, but I didn't even know what my own name meant!

"That's okay—you are too young to know ever-r-r-ything," Dorka says, smiling.

"Word, that's true, because nobody ever told me what my name means before," I say with a relieved laugh. In fact, everyone in the room laughs at my joke. Whew! Now I hope I can dance. Please, feet, don't fail me now.

While Dorka calls out the other girls' names, I start to think again about my name: Dorinda. God's gift. I wonder who named me that. Was it my real mother? If I was God's gift to her, then how come she gave me up?

I asked Mrs. Bosco once about her. Mrs. Bosco told me my "birth mother" was on a trip around the world. She must've gone around the world more than once, if you know what I'm saying, because that was seven years ago, and I'm *still* living at Mrs. Bosco's.

Flexing my ankle so it doesn't stiffen up on me now, I decide to go to the library after the audition and read some name books. I'm so nervous, I don't even hear what the other girls say about themselves, but like a zombie, I snap out of it when Dorka begins to give us the combinations to follow.

"Let's start in fifth position, right foot front. Move your foot to the side on *two*, then back on *three*, and close in first position on *four*," Dorka instructs us.

It's basically hip-hop style with jazz movements. I've got this covered on the easy-breezy tip.

But wait a minute . . . did she say back on two or three?

"Are you ready, girls?"

"Yes!" we answer in unison, and I quickly figure out that she had to have said 'on three.' The whole combination wouldn't make sense otherwise.

They're playing the MC Rabbit song "Can I Get a Nibble?"—which is straight-up hip-hop. I'm groovin' so hard, I don't even feel nervous anymore—until we're finished a few minutes later, and Dorka says, "Thank you, girls. If you've been chosen, you will receive a phone call. You were gr-e-a-t."

As I'm leaving, I say thank you to Dorka, since she knows Ms. Truly.

She smiles at me and says, "Good-bye, Dor-i-n-d-a!" That makes me feel like, well, "God's gift," if you know what I'm sayin'. She's so nice!

Chapter 6

As we are led back out by the giant in tights, I'm feeling dope about how the audition went. I worked it, Dorka liked me, and they all laughed at my joke. They won't forget my name, either.

Then, just like that, I feel like a wanna-be. I wonder why that is . . . Galleria and Chanel aren't like that at all—they never think of themselves that way. Even Aqua and Angie aren't exactly shy. A lot of times, I feel like I don't really belong with them at all. Like, with all my skills, I still don't feel like I got it like that.

Sometimes, I dream how they'll find out I'm twelve, and they'll think I'm wack, and a liar, and a fake, and they'll kick me out of the Cheetah Girls, and not be my crew anymore. . . .

As I come back out into the hallway, I can't believe there is still a long line of girls waiting to audition. They'll be here till the break of dawn.

Who am I kidding? There is no way I'll get picked for the Mo' Money Monique tour—no matter how dope I think my moves were. I'm only twelve. Look at how gorgeous these girls all are! Why did I even come here?

And then, I answer my own question. "I came here to prove to myself I could do it," I say. "And I did. I'm not a wanna-be—I'm a really good dancer, just like Ms. Truly said. Even though I have no chance at this job, I was great in there. And I'm as good a dancer as any of those other girls. *Better*."

I take a deep breath and exhale, smiling. All of a sudden, it doesn't matter anymore whether I get the job as a backup dancer, because right now, I feel like dancing till the break of dawn.

"Float like a butterfly and sting like a bee, all the way to the library," I hum to myself as I step outside onto Lafayette Street.

Maybe Ms. Truly is right. Maybe I should give up singing, which I'm just okay at, and stick to dancing. I do like singing though, even if I'm not that good. And I am getting better at it, thanks to Drinka Champagne's lessons.

Sitting down at a library desk, I settle down with the fattest name book I can find—*Boo-Boos to Babies Name Book*. Word. They have so many names in it from all around the world—and most of them I've never seen before.

Starting with the "A's," I decide to look up Arba's name, but I don't see it listed. Then I think, What about Topwe's name? I look it up . . . Here it is: "In southern Rhodesia, the topwe is a vegetable." I'd better not tell Twinkie, I think, 'cuz then she'll tease Topwe, and call him "Hedda Lettuce" or something. She is smart like that.

Then I see my name. Ms. Dorka is right. "Dorinda" means "God's gift." Ooh, look—the English variation of the name is "Dorothea." That's Bubbles's mom's name! Wait till I tell Bubbles that I have the same name as her mom!

Suddenly I get a pang in my chest. I *can't* tell Bubbles, because then she'll ask me how I met Dorka! It hits me full force that I'll never be able to tell my crew anything about my big audition! I'll never be able to say how Ms. Truly praised my dancing, or how I was brave enough to show up, and how I came through when it counted most. They'll never hear about Dorka.

It's a good thing I haven't got a chance at this job, I think with a laugh, 'cuz what would I tell them then? "Hey, y'all, I'm going on a 'round the world tour with Mo' Money Monique. See you later, cheetah-gators!"

I laugh at the thought of it. "Fat chance," I say, thinking of the hundreds of girls trying out for the job.

Hmmm . . . but there *is* a job I *can* possibly get, I think, remembering what Abiola told me.

Walking out of the library, I decide not to go home just yet. If I could get up the courage to go on the audition, then I can go downtown to see if I can get a job in the University Settlement's after-school program.

Being a Cheetah Girl is dope, but since our first gig, we haven't made any money at it, and the Apollo Amateur Night, while it's good exposure for us, doesn't pay either. Meanwhile, I need to start making *serious* loot.

Sure, we make a lot of our own outfits, but there are some things a Cheetah Girl just has to go out and buy. That's no problem for the rest of my crew. But as for me, my job at the YMCA concession stand doesn't pay enough, and I hate asking Mrs. Bosco for *anything*, because I know she can't afford it.

On the subway, I wonder again why my name is Dorinda. Did my real mom name me after someone? Why do I have a Spanish name? Nah, I can't be Spanish!

One thing is for sure—the receptionist at the University Settlement is *definitely* Spanish. "May I help you?" she asks, pushing her long, wavy black hair behind her ear.

"Um, I'm a freshman at Fashion Industries High School, and I want to apply for the after school work program," I say, feeling large and in charge now that I've been to a big audition for a job that pays a zillion times what this one does.

The pretty *señorita* hands me an application form and says, "You'll have to fill this form out, then someone will be right with you."

Word. I knew this would be on the easy-breezy tip. I'm in there like swimwear! Smiling from ear to ear, I sit down on the marble bench across from the receptionist to fill out my form.

"Excuse me, miss," the receptionist says to me.

I jump right up and go back to her window so she doesn't have to talk loud. Drinka says it's very bad for your vocal chords.

"You're going to need three pieces of identification. Do you have your birth certificate with you?" she asks me.

"No, I . . . didn't know I was supposed to bring it," I mutter, my face falling flat as a pancake.

"That's okay. You can fill out the form and leave it here, then come back with your ID when you have it," she says nicely. "You can see a job placement counselor any time from nine to five, Monday through Friday."

Where's the trapdoor in the floor when you need it? How am I gonna get out of this one?

"You know, I have to go home now anyway, because I have to baby-sit," I fib, but I'm so embarrassed because I know the receptionist *knows* I'm fibbing. She's probably wondering where my bib is!

Not batting an eyelash, the receptionist says,

"Sure, just come back another time, and bring your birth certificate, social security card, and a letter from one of your teachers. We just need proof that you're fourteen years old and attending school. You understand."

She knows I'm not fourteen! I walk out the door with my Cheetah tail between my legs. I walk past a big hole in the middle of Eldridge Street, where they're doing construction work. I wish I could just fall into that hole and disappear, and save everybody the trouble of having to put up with me!

Chapter
7

Mornings are always madness in my house, because all the kids try to get their breakfast at the same time, and "make some noise," like they're at a concert or something. Kenya is banging her spoon on the table. Topwe is playing his mouth like a boom box, and Twinkie is jumping up and down, trying to reach the knob on the cupboard over the sink.

"Twinkie, sit down, baby. I'm gonna get your cereal," Mrs. Bosco says, yawning and opening the cupboard. "Which box you want?"

"Oatmeal," Twinkie announces. In our house, there are no brand names with cute pictures of leprechauns or elves—just "no name," Piggly Wiggly supermarket stuff, with big black letters that say Corn Flakes, Rice, Beans and on and on till you could yawn.

"I want toast! I want toast!" Kenya yells, then thumps her elbow down on the counter.

"Kenya! *Can ya* please hush up!" Twinkie says, exasperated, causing all the kids to burst into a chorus of giggles.

"What's so funny?" Mrs. Bosco says, turning around to look at us, and pushing her bifocal glasses farther up her nose.

"Kenya, *can ya*, please hush up. Get it?" I volunteer.

"Oh." Mrs. Bosco chuckles, pouring the milk into Twinkie's cereal. "I'm sorry, Kenya, but you gonna have to have cereal today—so *can ya* please eat it before my nerves leave town?"

That's good for another round of hysterical giggles. Mrs. Bosco just smiles, and wipes her hands on a dish towel. "And y'all better hurry up, because we ain't got all day to get to school."

Kenya sticks her lip out as far as she can, then gets up from the table and storms out of the kitchen.

"I'll go get some bread. I'll be right back," I moan, then tell Kenya to come back to the table. I don't have time to fight with her today, even though she can be such a pain.

She doesn't say anything, but she does act like she feels a little guilty, so I can see that the little talk I had with her before bed last night must have made a difference. I explained to her how lucky we are to live here, and how sick Mrs. Bosco is, and how stealing kids' stuff at school isn't going to make her *any* friends.

I guess Mrs. Bosco was right, asking me to talk to her. The littler kids all listen to me—kinda like I was their mother or something. I don't think Mrs. Bosco would have wanted me to say anything about her being sick, but I said it anyway, and I'm not sorry. She needs us all to help her, not to get in her way. And whatever it takes to keep Kenya behaving, I'm going to do it.

As I'm slipping on my windbreaker hood, the phone on the kitchen wall rings. Mrs. Bosco answers it, then says, "Hold on a minute," before passing me the receiver.

"Who is it?" I ask, afraid.

"It sounded like she said 'Dokie Po' something," Mrs. Bosco says. She wrinkles her

forehead with a puzzled frown, causing
Topwe to burst out laughing.

"Oh, I know who it is," I say, because I don't
want to embarrass Mrs. Bosco.

"Hello?" I say nervously into the receiver.

"Dor-e-e-nda?" asks a strange voice with a
heavy accent.

"Yes," I answer cautiously, because I still
don't know who it is.

"It's Dorka Poriskova, the choreographer.
Dor-e-e-nda, I have good news for you."

Suddenly, I feel like someone could blow me
over with a peacock feather or something.
"Yes?" I ask in a squeaky voice.

"We want you for the Mo' Money Monique
tour. Rehearsal starts on Sunday morning at ten
o'clock. Can you make it?"

"I—I have to ask my mom," I stammer. What
I really want to do is scream for joy!

"Okay, but let us know today, because we
haven't much time to prepare before the tour
begins," Dorka says excitedly.

I am so numb when I put down the receiver,
for a second I don't hear Kenya's piercing voice
yelling at me to get her some toast.

I'm in such a daze, I just turn to Mrs. Bosco

and say, "They want me to tour with Mo' Money Monique as a backup dancer. . . ."

"Is that right?" Mrs. Bosco says, surprised, then wipes Topwe's crumb-infested mouth with a napkin. "Ain't that somethin', now!"

Stuffing my hands in my pockets, I stand motionless for a minute. How could they have picked *me*, out of all those dope dancers? There must be some kind of mistake, I tell myself, and they'll realize it as soon as they see me again. . . .

I start to feel a wave of panic creeping over me. I don't have time right now to even *think* about this. About leaving my family . . . my *crew* . . .

"You awright, baby? That's good news, right?" Ms. Bosco asks—'cuz she can see I'm not happy. She spills the orange juice in Topwe's cup, because she's so busy looking at me.

"Yeah," I say, my throat getting tight, like it does whenever I get nervous. "But I don't know if I wanna go."

What I *wanna* do is go back to bed and hide under the covers! I can't go to school and tell my crew *more* fib-eronis. So what *am* I gonna tell them?

I'd better bounce, I tell myself, so I can get to

school early and see Mrs. LaPuma, the freshman guidance counselor. I met with her when I first registered, and she was really nice. She told me if I ever had a problem, or needed career guidance, to come to her. Well, I guess I sure need it now!

I know I'm supposed to be happy, but all I feel is scared and confused, like that time my polka-dot dress came apart in school in sixth grade. It was the first dress I ever made, and I stayed up all night sewing it—by hand, since I didn't have a sewing machine yet.

I was so excited to wear it to school, but the seams started popping open by first period! I waited until everybody left the classroom before I got up and ran home. Everybody was laughing at me in the hallway.

I didn't go to school the next day, either. I was too embarrassed. Mrs. Bosco had to walk me to school herself the day after that, or I wouldn't have gone back even then!

"Can I help you?" asks the girl sitting at the front desk outside Mrs. LaPuma's office.

"Do you think Mrs. LaPuma could see me for a few minutes?" I ask her really nicely.

The girl's gold chains clank as she goes in to

ask Mrs. LaPuma, then they clank again as she walks back to her desk. "Mrs. LaPuma has a few minutes," she says. "Go on in."

I go inside, sit down by Mrs. LaPuma's desk, and tell her the whole drama.

"Well, Dorinda," she says when I am finished, "I think it would be good for you to go on the Mo'—what is her name?" Mrs. LaPuma asks, arching her high eyebrows even higher. I wonder how she draws them so perfect, 'cuz they both look exactly the same—like two smiley faces turned upside down and smiling at me.

"Mo' Money Monique. She's a *really* big singer right now," I explain, trying to impress Mrs. LaPuma so she won't think M to the M to the M sang at The Winky Dinky Lizard or something. "She has two songs on the chart right—"

"Yes, my daughter listens to rap music," Mrs. LaPuma says, cutting me off. She takes a sip of her iced coffee through a straw, leaving behind a red lipstick stain.

"Dorinda, I know how attached you feel to your friends, and your foster family. But this is a great opportunity for you. You deserve to try new experiences, dear, even at your young age.

Besides, if I may say so, it seems like you have your hands full at home. I know you may think you're not ready, but getting a break from your everyday life might be the best thing you ever did."

Mrs. LaPuma folds her hands on the desk, and looks at me for an answer. I sit there frozen, not knowing what to say. Why is Mrs. LaPuma trying to make it sound like I should run away from home?

"I'm not unhappy at home, Mrs. LaPuma," I try to explain, and I can feel my cheeks getting red because I'm getting upset. I don't want Mrs. LaPuma to tell Mrs. Tattle, my case-worker, that I was complaining or anything. See, I know that my teachers send reports about me to my caseworkers, since I'm legally a ward of the state.

"I'm not saying you are unhappy at Mrs. Bosco's, Dorinda," Mrs. LaPuma says sternly.

If there is one thing I hate, it's when grown-ups get that tone of voice like they know every-thing—and they don't!

"But what I *am* saying is, I don't think you realize what kind of daily strain you're under," Mrs. LaPuma goes on. "Being in a whole new environment, especially a creative one, may open up a whole world of new possibilities for you."

"I'm not trying to be funny, Mrs. LaPuma, but what strain am I under, washing dishes every night? It makes me feel good to help Mrs. Bosco. She's my *mother*. And the Cheetah Girls help me with *lots* of stuff."

"Dorinda, don't get so defensive," Mrs. LaPuma says, frowning. "The Cheetah Girls are wonderful, I'm sure—but you have to think about your *own* future. Being part of a major artist's tour, traveling around the world at your tender age . . ."

She sighs and leans forward, giving me a searching look. "I know that you're exceptionally bright, because I've looked at your junior high school records, but if it is your calling to be a dancer, then—"

At that moment, the girl with the musical jewelry comes in and interrupts us. "Mrs. LaPuma, may I speak to you a moment?" she asks, giving the guidance counselor a look.

"Excuse me for a moment, Dorinda," Mrs. LaPuma says, agitated. "Yes, what is it, Chloe?"

She follows the secretary into the outer office, and is gone for half a minute or so.

When she comes back in, she says hurriedly, "Dorinda, there's an emergency I have to attend to. We're a little short-staffed right, now so there is never a moment's peace around here. Good luck with your decision, and come back and see me if I can be of any further assistance."

"Oh, okay, bye, Mrs. LaPuma, thanks a lot," I say, getting up quickly in case she needs the chair. Emergency—yeah, right. I'll bet. The coffee machine is probably broken or something. Oh, well. I already got her point of view, and I know she's right—but I still feel really really bad.

Like it or not, it's show time. Time to see Bubbles and Chuchie before homeroom period. The three of us meet every morning, by the girls' lockers on the first floor. I hesitate now. How am I gonna tell them I got this job? They're gonna yell at me for not telling them sooner, and then—then, they're gonna talk me into *turning it down*! They're going to *hate* me!

Without even thinking, I walk over to the pay phone on the wall and deposit some change. I dial Ms. "Dokie Po," as my foster mother called her.

"Hi, Ms. Dorka, it's Dorinda Rogers. Yes. I just wanted to let you know that I'll be at rehearsal on Sunday. Yes. Ten o'clock. Thank you so much! Bye!"

Hanging up the phone, I feel instantly relieved. For better or worse, I've made my decision. There's no way for my crew to talk me out of it now.

I know Mrs. LaPuma is right. It'd be better for everybody if I just go away somewhere. Better for Mrs. Bosco. Better for the Cheetah Girls . . .

I mean, they don't need me, I tell myself. After all, Chuchie and Bubbles have each other, and Angie and Aqua have each other. Who do *I* have?

Besides, if this tour leads to more jobs, Mrs. Bosco can make room for some other foster child who needs a home. That's probably what Mrs. LaPuma was trying to say, but she was trying to be nice about it.

As I walk toward the lockers, I can see Chanel standing with her back turned, talking with Bubbles. Actually, I see Chanel's cheetah

backpack first, and suddenly I feel the butterflies fluttering in my stomach again. They are
the dopest friends I've ever had. How can I
leave them?

When Chanel turns around, I see she has red
scratches on her nose. I wonder if she and her
mother have been fighting or something. I
know Ms. Simmons is still upset with Chanel
for charging up her credit card.

"Where'd you get the scratches, Cheetah
Señorita?" I ask Chanel, trying to act normal.

"Kahlua's stupid dog Spawn did it," Chanel
sighs, then starts twirling one of her braids, like
she does whenever she gets nervous.

Kahlua is one of Chanel's neighbors. Chanel
doesn't like her, because she says she's stuck-
up, but since Kahlua has a dog and Chanel
doesn't, she visits her anyway. Chanel loves
dogs.

I ask, "What happened? Spawn caught you
drinking out of her bowl?"

"It's a *he*, Do' Re Mi," Chanel smirks. "And
where have you been?"

"Wh-what do you mean?" I stutter.
Suddenly, I can feel my cheeks turning red for
the second time today.

"I called you *twice* last night, and spoke to Mrs. Bosco for a long time," Chanel says, looking at me like I was a sneaky Cheetah.

"Word. She didn't tell me," I say, getting *really* nervous. I wonder what they talked about. And why didn't Mrs. Bosco tell me? Maybe she didn't *forget* to tell me. Maybe she didn't tell me for a reason!

"I talked to her, too," Bubbles says nonchalantly.

"You called, too?" I ask, squinching up my nose like I do when I'm confused. Sometimes the dynamic duo act like they are detectives or something.

"No, silly willy, we just did a three-way conference call," Bubbles says, flossing about her phone hookup.

Right now, I can feel something is happening on the sneaky-deaky tip, but I'm feeling too guilty to ask them what it is. These two are definitely up to *something*. If I'm lying, I'm frying!

"We have a surprise for you," Chanel says, then Bubbles pokes her.

"You're always blabbing your *boca grande*, Chuchie!"

"What kind of surprise?" I ask. I get the feeling

I'm being played like one of the contestants on "It's a Wacky World," who finds out they've won the wack booby prize.

"We'll tell you after school," Bubbles says, winking like a secret agent. Then she pulls out her furry Kitty Kat notebook, the one that she writes songs in, and scribbles something.

"Why don't you tell me at lunch?" I ask, trying to peep the situation.

That's when Bubbles and Chuchie give each other a look, and I *know* something is jumping off!

"Bubbles is gonna help me study for my Italian test. You know I'm not good at it, and I'm gonna fail if I don't study! So we can't meet you today at lunch, okay, *Señorita*?" Chuchie gives me a hug. "Don't be upset. We'll see you at three o'clock."

"I'm not trying to hear that, Chanel," I say— with an attitude, 'cuz now I am getting a little upset. "I know you two. You're up to something."

"You never answered our question," Bubbles says, butting in. "Where *were* you last night? How come you got home so late?"

"I, um, went to the library to study and I

couldn't take the books out 'cuz I owe too many," I say, trying to act on the easy-breezy tip.

"Yeah, right. What were you studying?" Chanel asks me, trying to act like Bobo Baboso again.

"Shoe design books and, um, I was reading this book about names and stuff," I volunteer.

"Names?" Bubbles asks, curious.

"Yeah," I say, exasperated, "*Boo-Boos to Babies Name Book.*"

Chuchie and Bubbles fall over each other giggling, then Bubbles stops laughing on a dime, and asks, all serious, "Do' Re Mi, is there something *you're* not telling us?"

All of a sudden, I feel like a frozen Popsicle got stuck to my tongue. They're just playing with me, 'cuz they already *know* about the Mo' Money Monique tour! Or even worse—they know I'm only twelve! Mrs. Bosco must have slipped and told them!

When Chuchie pats my tummy and bursts out laughing, I suddenly realize what they *really* mean. They *are* playing with me.

"I'm not picking out baby names, silly!" I blurt out. If they only knew that I'm twelve, and haven't even gotten my stupid period yet like they have, maybe they would stop laughing at me!

"Okay, Do' Re Mi, but a little fishy told me that you were playing 'hooky' with Red Snapper or Mackerel," Bubbles says, cackling just like a jackal!

Red Snapper and Mackerel are these two bozos who go to school with us, and seem to like Cheetahs, if you know what I'm saying. Their names are Derek Hambone and Mackerel Johnson, and they are ga-ga for Bubbles and Chanel.

They don't pay too much attention to me, which is good, 'cuz I'm not interested in them either. But that doesn't stop Bubbles and Chanel from teasing me about it.

"Yeah, well those fish had better keep swimming upstream, if you know what I mean," I say, playing back with Bubbles.

"Now *that's* the flava that I savor," Bubbles says, winking at me.

The three of us do the Cheetah Girls handshake. Then Bubbles and Chanel run off, screaming, "See ya at three, Do' Re Mi!"

I wave after them, my secret still a secret. But for how much longer?

Chapter
8

It's "five after three" and I'm trying not to "see what I see." My foster mother is standing right outside my school, right next to troublemaker Teqwila Johnson and her posse! What is Mrs. Bosco doing here, anyway? Something *must* be wrong.

I'm 'bout to bounce, but Mrs. Bosco sees me before I can make my move. "Hi, Mrs. Bosco," I say with a smile, trying to act normal.

I always call her Mrs. Bosco, even when we're in public, so kids don't make fun of how she looks. The first time she came to my school, I was in the first grade, and kids teased me the whole year, saying, "That's not *really* your mother! She's ugly!"

"What you are doing here?" I ask my foster mother nicely. Mrs. Bosco doesn't really like huggy, kissy stuff, especially in public, but I would really like to smooth the wrinkles down on her hot pink dress, which is shaped just like a tent.

"I just wanted to surprise you," Mrs. Bosco says, grinning from ear to ear.

Suddenly I feel sick to my stomach. I remember the day when I was almost five years old, and Mrs. Parkay was *really* nice to me for the first time. That was the very day the caseworker, Mrs. Domino, came to take me away.

"You're going to live with really nice people," she had said, as she held my hand and we crossed the street together. *Is that what Mrs. Bosco is gonna tell me now?* That I'm going to live somewhere else, with *"really* nice people?"

Well, I'm going away on tour with Mo' Money Monique, anyway, I remind myself. And I'll be gone a whole year. So it doesn't really matter whether she wants me or not. So there!

All of a sudden, I start to notice all the things about my foster mother that really bother me.

Like her false teeth, which she takes out at night, and puts in a glass of water on her dressing room table. And her thick mustache! Why can't she wax it off like most ladies do? And her really thick bifocal glasses!

And why didn't she wear the dope brown dress I made for her, with the big, oversized patch pockets in the front? Why couldn't she wear it to school if she really loves me?

I decide that I can't let Bubbles and Chanel see her—not looking like this. "I'm not gonna wait for Galleria and Chanel today, so we can leave now," I say to Mrs. Bosco, praying we can make it to the subway station before the dynamic duo come breaking out of school, which will happen any minute now.

"No, baby. I wanna see—I mean, meet your friends. You never bring them over to the house," Mrs. Bosco says, still smiling.

"I heard that!" Teqwila Johnson says loudly, letting out a big laugh like the stupid hyena she is. She whispers something to her friend Sheila Grand, whose last name fits her, because she's always acting like she's large and in charge.

Both of them are in my Draping 101 class,

and they never even talk to me. Now they must be making fun of me! I throw a cutting glance in their direction, but they pretend they're not looking at me.

All the people from my school are standing on the sidewalk, trying to act like they've got it going on. Fashion Industries is like that. We style and floss a lot.

All of a sudden I feel sad, like a wave washing over me. Suddenly, it doesn't matter that Mrs. Bosco isn't nice-looking, or that she dresses all frumpy. She's *real*—she never styles or flosses about anything. I don't wanna leave Mrs. Bosco, or Twinkie, or Arba.

And I don't wanna leave my crew, either. They're the dopest friends I've ever had in my whole life!

Just as I'm thinking all this, I hear, "Hi, Mrs. Bosco!" coming from my left side. It's Chanel, hiking up the waist on her pink plaid baggy jeans.

Wait a minute! How did she know this was my foster mother?

"Hi, Chanel. How you doin'?" Mrs. Bosco asks Chanel, like they've known each other their whole lives or something.

"Good. I just took a quiz in Italian class. I hope I pass it." Chanel giggles.

"Is that right?" Mrs. Bosco asks, acting all interested.

"Galleria made me switch from Spanish to Italian—but it's a lot harder," Chanel tells her.

"Y'all are matching," I say, pointing to Chanel's pants and Mrs. Bosco's dress.

"I know," Chanel says, smiling at Mrs. Bosco, then she even gives her a hug!

I can't believe it when Bubbles walks up and does the exact same thing to Mrs. Bosco! What's up with this situation?

Now *everybody* is looking at us. See, where there is Chanel and Bubbles, there is *mad* attention. Everybody is kinda jealous of them, because they're so pretty, and have the dopest style. Everybody knows we're in a group together, too, but I don't think anybody is jealous of me.

So what if they are, anyway? I don't care about that. All I wanna know is, what is this big surprise Chanel and Bubbles were flossin' about earlier? And how do they know Mrs. Bosco?

Picking up on my confusion, Chanel pipes

right in. "Do' Re Mi, *mamacita*, you are not gonna believe what we hooked up for you."

"That's the truth, Ruth," I say, squinting my eyes. This better be a good one.

"Princess Pamela has given the Cheetah Girls an all-day Pampering Pass at her Pampering Palace! Facials, pedicures, manicures, seaweed body wraps—the works, *mamacita*! We'll be so hooked up for the show at the Apollo, we'll win just because we look and feel so good, *está bien?*"

"Word!" I say in total surprise. So *this* is the big surprise the dynamic duo have been concocting! Mrs. Bosco was probably in on it, too—that's probably how she got hooked up with Bubbles and Chuchie. Now I feel stupid for being so worried.

"Can my mom come, too?" I ask my crew, calling her "mom" in front of everybody. I mean, Mrs. Bosco is always being nice to me, and here I've been acting like a spoiled brat, thinking about everything that's wrong with her. *She* deserves to go to Princess Pamela's—not me.

But my foster mom is not having it. "No, baby, I got too much to do around the house to be sitting up in some beauty parlor, like you girls. The only show I got to get ready for is the one I watch on TV," she says, chuckling. Then she suddenly starts coughing again. She doubles over, one hand over her mouth, the other on her chest.

It sounds like she's getting sick again. Please, I ask God, don't let her have to go back to the hospital! If she got sick again before I left on tour, I wouldn't go. I'd stay here and take care of her, I say, still praying.

And I guess my prayer is answered, 'cuz Mrs. Bosco stops coughing as fast as she started. She takes a deep breath. "Whoo," she says. "That's over. I feel better now. Uh, what were you tellin' me again?"

"Mrs. Bosco, I wuz sayin' that it's Princess Pamela's Pampering Palace—not just any beauty parlor, *está bien?*" Chanel says, giggling.

"Who is this Princess Pamela? She some kind of royalty?" Mrs. Bosco asks, amused.

"She's a gypsy," Bubbles chimes in.

"She's a psychic," Chanel continues.

"Well, she's a gypsy psychic gettin' paid," Bubbles adds. "I mean, she's got businesses all over the Big Apple. Princess Pamela's got growl power, and she doesn't even know it!"

"*And*, to top it all off, she's my father's girl-friend," Chanel flosses. She really loves Princess Pamela.

"What is growl power?" Mrs. Bosco asks, 'cuz now she is really finding my friends funny.

"That's when you really got it goin' on, and you got the brains, courage, heart—and busi-nesses—to prove it," Bubbles says. She loves to explain our whole vibe to anybody who asks—and everybody who doesn't.

"We'll get you to Princess Pamela's one day, Mrs. Bosco, you wait and see," Chanel says, laughing. "'Cuz you haven't lived until you've had a Fango Dango Mud Mask, *está bien?*"

"The passes are for a full day treatment, plus a free touch-up the week after. So if we go with the flow this Saturday right after Drinka's, we can get our touch-ups next Saturday afternoon, right before our show at the Apollo. We'll be lookin' so phat, we're bound to make people sit up and take notice," Bubbles finishes, flossing for Mrs. Bosco's sake.

That makes me a little uncomfortable. I mean, getting to perform one song in the Apollo Amateur Hour isn't exactly a show, if you know what I'm saying—not like doin' a whole world tour with Mo' Money Monique.

I give Mrs. Bosco a quick look. Did I warn her not to say anything about the tour to my friends? I can't remember! I've got to get her out of here, quick, before she starts blabbing about it. I know I'm going to have to tell my crew eventually, but not yet—not now! I'm not ready to face their reaction. No way!

"Why you calling yourself fat, baby?" Mrs. Bosco says to Bubbles, misunderstanding. "You so pretty, and there ain't nothing wrong with a little meat and potatoes."

We all start laughing so hard, *everybody* is looking at us—including Derek Hambone and Mackerel Johnson.

"Mrs. Bosco, *phat* doesn't mean fat—it means *dope*," Chanel tries to explain, confusing my foster mother even more. This sends us all into fits of giggles again.

"It means, like, fabulous," Bubbles adds, sounding like her mom, Dorothea—my name-sake.

Now the Mackerel and the Red Snapper have worked their way over to us, and are standing behind Bubbles, listening to our conversation!

I'm trying to get Bubbles's or Chanel's attention, but they aren't looking at me.

"Oh, I understand, baby. You girls are so smart, with all your words. Dorinda is always telling me some new words y'all made up," Mrs. Bosco says, fixing her bifocal glasses again.

"Hey, Cheetah Girls, what's the word for the day?" Derek busts in, trying to cash in his two cents.

"Cute but no loot, Red Snapper," Bubbles says, but nicer than she usually talks to Derek-probably because my foster mother is standing right there.

"Come on with it, Kitty Kat, and show me where the money's at!" Derek says, slapping his boy Mackerel a high five, like he's saying something.

"See ya, *schemo*, we gotta bounce," Bubbles says, then motions for Chanel to walk with her.

Mackerel and the Red Snapper follow them for a while, then give up and walk away. I'm so relieved that I didn't have to introduce them to Mrs. Bosco.

Not that I'm ashamed of her—I'm not. But

still, I don't want everybody at school to know my business. My private life is private, you know what I'm sayin'? Why should they even know I have a foster family, not a real one? I mean, not even my crew knows everything about me, right?

Bubbles and Chanel are off to Toto in New York. I'm alone with my foster mother now, and she's being really quiet. Unusually quiet. I wonder what's up with her. "Are you okay?" I ask, scared. "You're not getting sick again, are you?"

"No, baby, I'll be all right. Doctor says all's I need is rest."

"Rest? You never rest," I say, worried.

"Don't worry 'bout me," she says. "I'll be all right. Long's I have my nap every afternoon . . ."

"But how will you do that when I'm on tour?" I ask. "Who's gonna look after Kenya and all them?"

"Monie will have to help out. She's been spending too much time with that Hector anyway. Don't you worry, baby, like I said. You go off on your tour and don't even think about us."

Yeah, right. "Here. Let me hold that bag."

"Awright, child." Mrs. Bosco hands me the Piggy Wiggly shopping bag, but it's really heavy.

"What's in here?" I ask.

"Q-Tips," Mrs. Bosco says, chuckling at her little joke. See, she uses Q-Tips dipped in peroxide to clean Corky's ears, 'cuz she says he must be hard of hearing. She always yells at him, "Why else do I have to tell you to pick up your socks and pants fifty times and you *still* don't do it?"

We're almost to the subway entrance now, and I start thinking again about why Mrs. Bosco is being so quiet. And how my friends all acted like they knew her, when I know I made sure they never got to come to my house.

Something is definitely going on, I can feel it. And if it isn't about Mrs. Bosco's health, then what is it?

As if she can hear my thoughts, Mrs. Bosco stops at the bottom of the subway steps and turns to face me. "How would you feel about me and Mr. Bosco adopting you?" she asks all of a sudden.

We've never talked about this before. Never. When I first got to her house, she told me that my birth mother might come back to get me at anytime, so I shouldn't get too attached to her or Mr. Bosco—but that she would always be my second mom.

I wonder why she's asking me this now? "I don't know how I feel about it," I say. This is making me really nervous. "What about my, um, *real* mother?" I ask her, but I'm looking down at my shoes. I can feel my whole body shaking.

"Well, I'm just asking you a question. If I could adopt you, would you want me to?" Mrs. Bosco repeats, coughing into a tissue. She always loses her breath when we have to go up or down subway stairs.

"But what about the money you get from foster care for taking care of me?" I ask nervously. I don't want Mrs. Bosco to have to stop getting her foster care checks, just to adopt me. I know she loves me anyway. I wouldn't want to cost her that money.

"Don't worry about that," Mrs. Bosco says. Then she puts her arm around my shoulder and leans in toward me. She always used to do this when I was little, and I know exactly what she is going to say.

"I know when you grow up, we gonna go live in a big ole fancy house together, with a whole lot of bedrooms—'cuz you always had the smartest head on your shoulders."

Now I *do* smooth down the crease that's riding up in the front of dress, and she lets me, too. "Yeah," I say.

"Yeah, what," Mrs. Bosco asks.

"Yes! Yes, I want to be adopted!"

"Awright, baby," she says with a sweet smile. "I'll see what I can do, but I can't promise you anything—'cuz you know how trifling those people can be."

"Those people" are what my foster mother calls everyone who works at the Department of Child Welfare, Division of Foster Care Services, which is a big, dingy office in downtown Manhattan. I go once a year for psychological testing, and to visit my social worker, Mrs. Carter. She is in charge of all the caseworkers who make visits in the field.

"Do you really want me to go on tour with Mo' Money Monique?" I ask my foster mother.

"If that's what you want to do, that's fine with me, Dorinda. You always was dancing around the house, even when you wuz little. I know you got your new friends, and you don't wanna leave them—but you got to do what's right for you. You know I always say, ain't nuthin' wrong with Mo' Money!"

Mrs. Bosco puts her arm through mine, and leads me onto the subway platform. "But if you're not ready to go off around the world and be a working girl, don't worry 'bout that, either," she says. "After all, we got plenty of time to go live in that big ole mansion somewhere."

Suddenly, I feel like crying. It's almost too good to be true. Me—adopted after all these years, with Mr. and Mrs. Bosco as my real parents. And going on tour with Mo' Money Monique!

I guess Monie the meanie will have to finally help out for a change. And I guess the Cheetah Girls will have to carry on without me.

I wonder if I'll still be around for the Apollo Amateur Night. I mean, the tour probably won't leave town that soon, right? Maybe I can get away with not telling my crew about the tour until after we perform at the Apollo. That way, I can still be a Cheetah Girl for just a little longer.

The Cheetah Girls

I like this new plan of mine. Sure, it means I have to keep my secret for a whole 'nother week. But it's worth the stress. I mean, what if I go to rehearsal tomorrow, and it turns out there was a big mistake, and I didn't really get the job after all? You know what I'm sayin'? Or what if I mess up so bad at the rehearsal that they fire me? I'd be so embarrassed if I'd already told my crew about my big new job!

Besides, I figure, the longer I don't tell them, the better. 'Cuz once I do, the Cheetah Girls are really gonna pounce. They'll probably never even speak to me again!

Chapter 9

When you're standing on the corner of 210th Street and Broadway, you'd think that Princess Pamela owns the whole block or something. Both of her businesses—Princess Pamela's Pampering Palace, and Princess Pamela's Poundcake Palace—take up several doorways on each side.

The Pampering Palace is really the bomb. It's got a glittery ruby red sign outside, with stars, balls, and moon shapes hanging in the window.

"The stars, moon, and planets are supposed to symbolize another galaxy—'cuz that's where you are when you step inside the Palace," Chanel explains to us proudly.

When you walk in the Palace, you feel like

you're taking a magic carpet ride, because everything is covered in red velvet, and the floor is covered with red carpet! When I look up at the ceiling, there are all these chandeliers that look like crystal drops falling from the sky! It's the dopiest dope place I've ever been—besides Bubbles's mom's store, Toto in New York.

"Close your mouth!" Bubbles instructs Angie, who is as awestruck as I am by the Princess's Palace. It's a diggable planet look, all right.

"Ah, my boot-i-full Chanel and her friends!" Princess Pamela says, rushing to greet us with open arms. She goes over to Chanel and starts crushing her to death. I wish my foster mother would hug me like that. Maybe once she really adopts me, she will. . . .

When you put the P to the P, Princess Pamela looks just like a gypsy psychic lady is supposed to. She is really pretty, and she has dark, curly hair streaked with white in the front. Her eyebrows are dark and thick, and she has a red, red mouth. She probably doesn't eat baloney and cheese sandwiches like I do, because she has to keep her lipstick looking so dope.

"Is that rayon crushed velvet?" I ask Princess Pamela, goggling at all the yards it must have taken to make her dress, which is sweeping to the floor like Cinderella's gown.

"Yes, dahling. You like?" Princess Pamela asks me, her big brown eyes twinkling. "I know where you can get an *excellent* price on velvet. Let me know if you want to go, dahling."

"Awright, 'cuz I'd be hooked up if I had a dress like that," I tell her.

"You, dahling, are so boot-i-full, like my little Chanel, that you could wear nothing but a leaf, and e-v-e-r-y-o-n-e would be *green* with Gucci Envy!" she says, pinching my cheeks. Usually I hate when grown-ups do that, but she's so cool, I don't mind.

You can tell Chanel is proud of Princess Pamela by the way she beams with pride at the Princess's jokes.

The receptionist, who has a hairstyle that looks more like a "boo-boo" than a bouffant, tells us in this heavy British accent to "go back and change into your robes and slippers in the dressing room, and someone will be with you in a jiffy." Then she starts sneezing into a tissue, and her eyes are watering like she's crying.

"Is the English lady sick?" I ask Princess Pamela. I don't know the lady's name, but I don't want to call her a receptionist, in case she turns out to be royalty, or something.

"No, she has allergies, dahling, and she's not from England. She's from Idaho," Princess Pamela whispers, putting her arm around me.

"Then why does she talk like that—with an accent?" I ask, puzzled.

"When you're from a place named after a potato, you have to do something to make yourself interesting, no?" Princess Pamela says, smiling mischievously. Now I see why Chanel loves her. Princess Pamela's got mad flava.

"Okay, Mademoiselle Do' Re Mi, what will it be?" Bubbles asks, whipping out the beauty menu like she's a French waiter. "Le lavender mousse conditioning body scrub, or le pepper-mint pedicure?"

"Gee, Bubbles, I never really thought about it," I quip. "But now that you mention it, I would like a cherry sundae back rub!"

"You're a mess, Dorinda!" Aqua heckles me. Then she turns to Galleria and asks, "You think they got anything for athlete's foot? All these dance classes are giving me fungus right in between my toes. See right there." Aqua holds up her foot so Bubbles can get a good view.

"If I were you, I wouldn't be worried about fungus 'till I took care of those *Boomerang* toes, Aqua," Bubbles says, holding her nose closed like something stinks. "I mean, you got any hot dogs to go with those corn fritters?"

"That's all right, I'm not mad at you," Aqua says. "But I sure hope they got something for them."

Seriously studying the beauty menu, Bubbles exclaims, "Aqua, look, it says here that a tea tree oil bath is such a powerful antiseptic, it will even get rid of the cock-a-roaches between your toes!"

"Lemme see that menu, 'cuz I know it does not say that," Angie says, coming to the defense of her twin sister.

Angie is the more "chill" of the two, but sometimes the Walker twins are so much alike I can't tell them apart—especially now that they are wearing matching red velvet robes and slippers.

I wish I had a twin sister like that. A *real* sister, anyway. Someone who'd stick up for me. When I turn around from putting my robe on, I catch Bubbles, Chanel, and the twins whispering together.

"Don't be making fun of me!" I say, wincing. "So what if the robe *is* really big on me!"

My crew looks at me all serious, and Aqua says, "What makes you think we wuz talking about you anyway, Dorinda?"

"'Cuz I know you four. You'll read me through the floor," I say. Aqua never calls me by my nickname, Do' Re Mi, but I like the way she says Dorinda, because it sounds cute with her southern drawl.

"Well, we have a special treat for you, Miss Dorinda," Bubbles says.

All of a sudden, an attendant appears, in a white uniform and white shoes, with a white towel draped around her arm. She looks like a nurse in a cuckoo hospital, and I'm beginning to feel like a cuckoo patient.

"Could you come with me, *mademoiselle*?" she says, looking at me.

Princess Pamela's place is like the United Nations, I think to myself. Kinda like my house. But I think the French nurse's accent is real, and I'm not sure I wanna go anywhere with her.

"Not having it," I moan, looking right at Bubbles, who is probably the ringleader behind this whole situation.

"Come on, Dorinda, we're going with you, too," Aqua volunteers. They all escort me to a room with red velvet walls, and a long, pod-shaped tub that looks really weird.

"What's this for?" I ask the French nurse lady.

"It is for *ze cell-yoo-lete* treatment, *mademoiselle*," she explains to me.

"*Mademoiselle* doesn't want any treatment," I say, looking at Angie and Aqua, and not even trying to pronounce whatever that word was she said.

"Dorinda, that's the whole idea. This is so you won't get any cellulite," Aqua pipes in.

"How am I gonna get something that I don't even know what it is?" I exclaim, sucking my teeth. How did Aqua know what it is, anyway? She's such a show-off.

"Cellulite is that lumpy cottage-cheese-looking stuff that girls get on the back of their thighs," Aqua says, pointing to her butt.

If I didn't know any better, I'd swear Aqua and Angie are making this stuff up as they go along. "Where's Bubbles and Chanel?"

"They're in the, um, other—" Angie hems and haws.

"Super cellulite treatment room," Aqua joins in.

"Please try, *mademoiselle*," the attendant begs me.

"Okay, but *mademoiselle* doesn't like this one bit," I moan, giving in to what I have a feeling is somebody's idea of a Cheetah Girl joke.

"You have to stop talking now, *mademoiselle*," the French lady whispers in my ear. "For all of the impurities to leave your body, it requires absolute silence."

She wraps this Saran Wrap stuff around me—so, so tight that I swear *I'll* be leaving my body soon. Then she seals me in the pod, and turns on a dial. Just what I need. Some science project experiment gone wrong!

I lie there, wrapped in plastic like a sandwich in the fridge. Suddenly, I feel real sleepy, like my body is being deprived of oxygen or something. As I doze off, I swear to myself, if I grow up and have cellulite after this, I'm gonna sue—guess who!

When I wake up, I'm the only one in the room

with the French nurse lady, who peers up her nose at me over her little glasses. When I get some more duckets, I'm gonna buy Mrs. Bosco nice little glasses like that.

Yawning, I wonder how long I've been in this "invasion of the body snatcher" pod, but I'm definitely ready to bust out.

"C'est bien, mademoiselle?"

"No, *mademoiselle* is not all right." I moan. At least that gets her hopping like a hare, and soon, I'm out of the baggie. I'm so happy to be back in a robe, just chilling.

But before I know it, the nurse has covered my face with a gucky banana-cream facial mask, and my eyes are covered with cucumber slices! I'm beginning to feel like an appetizer, if you know what I'm saying!

"Now what?"

As I try to recline in the chair and relax, I wonder—why am I always in a room by myself? I thought this was supposed to be fun. You know, the Cheetah Girls sitting around in some big bubble bath all day, talking and giggling.

Why do ladies do all this stuff, anyway? It's *boring*. I don't know how long I'm leaning back in the reclining chair, looking like a moonpie, before I finally hear the voice of the mischievous one.

"Do' Re Mi, can't you see how boot-i-full you look?" says Galleria. The nurse removes the cucumber slices, and I see Bubbles, Chanel, Aqua, and Angie standing over me, giggling.

"Was I sleeping again?" I ask them. I'm so annoyed, I don't think I'm ever gonna get a facial, or even wash my hair, ever again.

"Like Sleeping Beauty," Chanel says.

"It's time to bounce," Bubbles says, standing by while the French lady helps me off the table and hands me a glass filled with bubbles.

"This will help replenish your epee-dermis," advises the French lady.

"What's an epee-dermis?" Angie asks.

"It's the top layer of your chocolate skin, missy," Bubbles explains.

"Ooh, epidermis," Angie says, sucking her teeth. "We don't just sit around and sing all day at school, Galleria. Sometimes we have classes, and study things like *biology*."

"Let's all go over Dorinda's house, and eat popcorn, and watch *Scream*," Aqua says, interrupting her sister—and looking straight at *moi*.

"Are you crazy? The only 'scream' you two are gonna see at my house is all my brothers and sisters doing it for real," I say, rolling my eyes.

"Well, we already called your—um, Mrs. Bosco, and she says it's okay if we come over," Angie volunteers.

"No way," I say, looking at all four of them like I'm gonna pounce. "We're not going over my house."

"*Sí, sí*, Do' Re Mi," quips Chanel. "We're there, baby!"

"Word, I don't know what y'all have been drinking, but I'm not having it, okay?" I say, changing back into my clothes—*finally*!

Chapter 10

When we finally get outside on Broadway, Bubbles announces that we're taking a taxi, because we're late.

"Late for what?" I ask.

"Um . . . you know that show we watch on television?" Aqua chimes in. "Aqua—what's the name of that show we watch on Saturdays?"

"Dag on, don't *poke* me," Angie whines, rubbing her arm. "I can't remember."

"Taxi!" Bubbles yells loudly. She runs to the curb, and waves her hand in the air.

In the Big Apple, the yellow taxis fly by faster than Can Man with his shopping cart. I've been practically run over by them more than once. But Bubbles knows what she's doing. She

stands on the edge of the curb, waving and tilt-
ing way forward. Then she quickly leans back
whenever a car zips by. A real native New
Yorker.

"Let's take a 'gypsy' cab!" Chanel giggles,
making a joke on Princess Pamela, but Aqua
and Angie don't get it.

"What's a gypsy cab?" asks Aqua, squinching up her nose. We all heckle. We love to tease
Aqua and Angie because they're kinda, well,
southern. They've only been in New York since
last summer, and they don't know the ways of
the Big Apple.

Chanel explains the gypsy snap to her, and
then Bubbles explains what a gypsy cab *really*
is: "The seats are always dirty in the back, and
they always have some smelly pine freshener
stinking up the whole car. You only take 'em
when you're desperate, or when your hairdo is
gonna flop from the sopping rain."

"Oh," Aqua says, nodding her head, then
laughs, "How you know 'Freddy' or 'Jason'
ain't driving the cab, though?"

"'Cuz they wouldn't pick *you* up!" I throw
in. "They'd be too scared of you, the way you
two scream!"

We all start screaming—"Aaahhh!"—imitating Aqua and Angie last Halloween, when they screamed so loud, all the kids were scared of *them*.

"We're in!" Bubbles says, motioning us to hop in a yellow taxi. Since we're heading downtown from 210th Street, the first stop is gonna be my house on 116th Street. Then the taxi can keep going downtown and drop off the twins at 96th Street before taking Bubbles and Chuchie home.

When the taxi pulls up in front of the Cornwall Projects, though, Bubbles, Chanel, Aqua, *and* Angie jump out, and hightail it to the entrance of Building A, where I live.

"Come on, y'all, I already told you—you can't come to my house," I whine, slamming the taxi door. How'd they know which building I lived in, anyway?

"Oh yes we can, *Señorita*, 'cuz Mrs. Bosco invited us. *Está bien?*" Chanel says, leaping along like a ballerina.

Suddenly I realize the danger I'm in. Never mind that my house is small and crowded. What if my foster mother slips, and says something about the Mo' Money Monique tour?

Mrs. Bosco probably thinks I've already told my crew about it.

Panicking, I run as fast as I can to warn her, but Chanel is hanging on to my jacket for some reason. I pull at it, trying to get free. I can't have my secret come out. Not yet!

"Do' Re Mi, we don't care if you don't live in a palace. Leave that to Princess Pamela!" Chanel says. Then she gives me a *really* tight hug, while ringing my bell with her free hand.

"Chanel! Let go of me!" I giggle. "Why are you ringing my doorbell when I have keys?"

Mrs. Bosco opens the door, and me and Chanel fall on top of her. Except, I'm not so sure it's my foster mother. It doesn't really *look* like her. She looks . . . *better*, if you know what I'm saying.

"Hi, baby, we've been waiting for you."

I would know that voice in a tunnel. It's my foster mother, all right—and if I still had any doubts, she starts coughing into a tissue.

But look at the pretty flowered dress she's wearing. And I like her new wig—it's nothing fancy, just a nice soft brown, with curls.

And she's wearing *makeup*! My foster mother *never* wears makeup.

Now I know why she looks so different. She doesn't have a mustache anymore!

"Mrs. Bosco, you look *really* nice," I say.

Bubbles starts heckling. "You should have seen what we had to go through to wax her mustache!"

This sends everyone into a fit of giggles. "We told her we had a surprise for her, *está bien?*" exclaims Chanel. "Then we blindfolded her, and Bubbles put the wax on her upper lip— then pulled it off while me, Angie, and Aqua held her down!"

"When did you do all that?" I ask, surprised.

"While you wuz getting cell-yoo-leeted!" Angie says, beside herself with laughter.

Then I look around at the crowd of people in the living room. I hadn't noticed them all at first—and they start yelling, "Surprise!"

I mean, all of my brothers and sisters— including Monie the Meanie—Dorothea and her husband, Mr. Garibaldi, Ms. Simmons, and even some people I don't know! Everyone is standing around like they're at a party. Even Mrs. Gallstone from down the hall is here.

I *really* don't get whazzup with this situation. I mean, it's not my birthday. And then it hits me. Oh, no! *They already know my secret!*

If I wasn't so young, I think I would have a heart attack. My heart is beating so fast, I'm still not sure I won't be the first twelve-year-old to have one—and get written up in the *Guinness Book of World Records*. I'm not lying.

Mrs. Bosco must have told everybody that I'm going on the Mo' Money Monique tour! That's what this party is all about! I could just scream. How could she do this without asking me? I'd like to read her right now!

But instead of saying what I want to say, I hear myself blurting out, "Look at all the pretty flowers."

Then my eyes feast on the long banquet table that Mrs. Bosco always borrows from Mrs. Gallstone when we have a party. It's filled with all my *favorite* foods—fried chicken, potato salad, collard greens, rice and beans, black-eyed peas, corn bread, and one, two, *seven* sweet potato pies! Too bad I'm not the least bit hungry.

But wait a minute. If everybody knows I'm going on tour, how come they're not all upset? They're being so nice, even though I'm leaving them.

I feel so sad. Look at all the trouble they went

to for me! And I was about to yell at them! I flop down in a kitchen chair, like a scarecrow stuffed with straw. I don't deserve all of this. I feel so stupid—like Chanel did when she got caught using her mother's credit card.

"You and my mom did all this?" I ask, looking at Bubbles, Chanel, Aqua, and Angie.

"Yep. The body snatcher contraption was Princess Pamela's idea. We got you *good*," Aqua says proudly. "And me and Angie helped Mrs. Bosco cook all this dee-licious food just for you."

"Oh, no, honey—it's for us, too," Angie counters, "'cuz you know I'm hungry after all that tea tree oil!"

"Ah, ah, ah, don't forget about my Italian pastries," Mr. Garibaldi adds, waving his hand.

"Yeah, that's right. Dad made Chuchie's favorite—chocolate-covered cannolis!" Bubbles says, beside herself.

I heave a huge sigh. All this beautiful food. Too bad I'm not the least bit hungry. In fact, I feel sick about everything.

I look around the room, and I see people I don't even know. Who is this tall man with a mustache? Who is the tall woman with the

African fabric draped around her, and a turban that almost touches the ceiling?

The man catches my look. "Dorinda, I've heard so much about you from my daughters, and I'm quite honored to be here. I'm Mr. Walker," he says, extending his hand to me.

"Oh," I say smiling. It's Aqua and Angie's father. He looks like a successful businessman, all right.

"And this is my girlfriend, Alaba."

She looks like a model from some African tribe or something. I wonder what her name means? I'll have to look it up in the *Boo-Boo* name book. Aqua is behind her, making a face.

Galleria isn't finished talking. She puts a hand on my shoulder, and points the other one at my foster mom. "I want you to know that, even though we helped put it together, throwing the adoption party was always Mrs. Bosco's idea."

Adoption party? Did Bubbles say adoption party?

Now I need *my* ears poked with a Q-Tip dipped in peroxide, 'cuz I must be hard of hearing, like Corky. "Did you say, 'my adoption party'?"

"Mrs. Bosco has adopted you, silly willy Do' Re Mi!" Bubbles blurts out.

So *that's* why Mrs. Bosco was asking me all that stuff by the subway the other day. And that's how they all knew each other—they were planning this whole party together, complete with the visit to Princess Pamela's to get me out of the way!

I burst into a round of tears that would make the Tin Man in *The Wizard of Oz* squeak. Mrs. Bosco has *already* adopted me! I have a *real mom*!

"Dorinda, look at you, you're going to ruin all the effects of that delicious banana cream pie facial mask!" Dorothea says. Coming over to hug me, she pulls a leopard-print tissue out of her pocketbook. I notice that she's crying, too. "You don't know how happy I am for you," she says.

"Thank you, Ms. Dorothea," I say through my tears. I look across the room at my crew, who are all beaming at me. They all love me, I can see that. Look at the trouble they went to for my sake. How can I keep on lying to them?

I can't.

"I'm so sorry to be leaving all of you," I say.

"Huh?" Ms. Dorothea says. "What's this about leaving?"

"It won't be forever," I say. "Just for a year. As soon as the tour is over, I'll be back, and we'll be better than ever, I promise."

"Tour? What tour?" Galleria asks, looking at me, puzzled.

That *really* makes me start bawling like a crawling baby.

"Dorinda is a crybaby! Dorinda is a crybaby!" Kenya says, sucking her teeth.

"Kenya, *can ya* please hush up for a second," Mrs. Bosco says, putting her finger to her mouth.

"What tour?" my crew says in unison.

I just blurt out my whole confession, all at once. I tell them about the trail of lies I told to cover up my big audition, and about the rehearsal tomorrow.

Suddenly I feel everybody's eyes staring at me. Behind Alaba, I see Angie and Aqua looking stunned. And Chanel looks like she just got hit on the head with a brick.

They all turn to Galleria, waiting to see how she's gonna react. I look at her, too. She's our leader. Whatever she says, goes. If she says I'm

123

out, then that's it. I lower my eyes, waiting for the verdict.

"Don't let us stop you from making 'Mo' Money,' Do' Re Mi. If you want to go on tour, you *go*," Bubbles says proudly. She looks at the rest of our crew as if she's answering for all of them. "We're proud of you for getting such a big gig. And don't worry—we'll always take you back as a Cheetah Girl, even if you come back when you're a hundred! Ain't that right, girls?"

"Right!" they all shout, gathering around me.

That gets me crying again, and I feel *really* bad, because now I don't know what to do about anything! I love my family and my crew so much—how can I bear to leave them?

"Are you happy about it?" Bubbles says, kneeling down next to me and holding my hand.

"I don't know. I don't wanna leave y'all now," I mumble.

"No, I mean about being adopted. You said you always dreamed about being adopted, and now it's happening. Dorinda, it's your dream come true."

Before I can answer Galleria, Ms. Dorothea suddenly bursts into tears! She runs out of the living room, her peacock boa dropping feathers behind her.

"Mom, what's wrong?" Bubbles turns around to look, but all she sees is the flurry of feathers falling to the floor, like snowflakes.

Dorothea locks herself in the bathroom, and she won't come out. After what seems like, well, forever, me and my crew and Ms. Simmons put our ears to the bathroom door.

"Ms. Dorothea is still crying," Angie whispers.

I feel terrible. "Do you think it's something I said?"

"No, Dorinda, I think Dorothea has always been a little dramatic," Ms. Simmons says.

She should talk. That "off-Broadway performance," as Bubbles called it, that Ms. Simmons pulled when Chanel got caught charging on her card would have sent the Wicked Witch of the West flying away on her broomstick!

"Ms. Dorothea, can I come in?" I yell through the keyhole.

"Only if you come in by yourself," Dorothea says, sniffling, then bawling again.

Bubbles looks at me like, "Whazzup with that?" But she has to understand that she can't always take care of everything.

"I'll handle this," I whisper, then knock softly on the door.

"Dorinda, I'm so glad we can talk by ourselves," Dorothea says, sniffling and laughing after she's closed the door behind us. "Sorry we have to meet like this," she says, balancing herself on the edge of the bathtub.

I feel embarrassed because the paint has chipped off, but Mr. Hammer, the super, keeps saying he's going to repaint it soon. I wish my apartment was dope like hers, with cheetah stuff everywhere.

"You know, Dorinda," she says, sniffling into her tissue, "from the first time I met you, I felt close to you."

"I know, Ms. Dorothea. I feel close to you, too," I reply.

"Now I know why," she says, pausing, then pulling down her leopard skirt over her knees. "I, um, I, um, always wanted to be adopted, too." Then she starts bawling again.

"You were a foster child?" I ask, amazed. "Bubbles never told me that."

"Bubbles doesn't know," Ms. Dorothea says, smiling at her daughter's nickname. "I never told her."

"Oh," I say, then we both hug. I would never have known Ms. Dorothea was a foster child. She is so beautiful and everything.

"I've hired a private detective to help find my mother, but I'm not having much luck," she says, sobbing some more.

So that's why she hired a detective! I think, remembering Bubbles and Chuchie's conversation in the chat room that night. "Oh, I'm sorry, Ms. Dorothea," I say, comforting her. "Don't give up, you'll find her."

"Maybe, maybe not," Dorothea says, then pauses. "Do you know what happened to your birth mother?"

"No. Um, Mrs. Bosco says she went on a trip around the world or something, but I don't know." I'm whispering, because I don't want anyone to hear me through the door. "I never told anybody that. Not even them."

Pointing outside the door, Ms. Dorothea smiles. "Well, let's just keep this our little secret, okay?"

"Okay. I won't say anything."

"I'm not ready to tell Galleria about my childhood. I never told her, because I've always wanted her to have a perfect life. But watching you just now, telling the truth, I felt so proud, like you were *my* daughter. One of these days, I'm gonna tell Galleria the truth—she deserves to hear it."

"Yes, she does," I agree.

"And you, Dorinda—now you have two mothers, whether you like it or not, okay? Mrs. Bosco—and me."

"Yes, Ms. Dorothea," I say. Now I'm crying harder than ever, and she holds me for what seems like hours. Then I remember about our names.

"Did you know that Dorothea and Dorinda are both variations of the same name—meaning 'God's gift?'"

"No, I didn't know that," Dorothea says, wiping her eyes with what's left of her tissue. Then she starts laughing uncontrollably. "God's gift—wait till Ms. Juanita hears that one!"

We're still laughing when I open the bathroom door, but Dorothea wants to stay in there for a while longer, so I go out by myself. Of course, Bubbles, the rest of my crew, and Ms. Juanita are still standing outside the door—being nosy posy, no doubt.

Who's 'Bout to Bounce?

"What were y'all laughing about?" Bubbles says.

"I told her that my name and her name both mean 'God's gift.'"

"Really?" Bubbles exclaims.

"No wonder she's so conceited!" Juanita says, huffing.

"I wonder what *your* name means!" I heckle, then the six of us huddle outside the bathroom door, hugging and giggling together.

"We should leave her alone in the bathroom for a while," I say, pushing everyone toward the living room.

"That's for sure, 'cuz she wouldn't be caught dead crying and then not fixing her makeup!" Juanita chimes in.

Bubbles gives us a look behind Juanita's back, then blurts out, "Neither would *you*, Auntie Juanita!"

Chapter 11

Yesterday I may have been adopted, but today, nothing has changed in my house. Mrs. Bosco is washing dishes. Topwe is fighting with Kenya over the last slice of sweet potato pie, and Monie the Meanie is still here, talking on the phone with her boyfriend Hector. "Shut up!" she screams at the other kids. "Can't you see I'm talking?"

I don't pay much attention, though. I've got bigger things on my mind. Today is do-or-die day. I'm going to my first rehearsal for the Mo' Money Monique tour. Not only are the butterflies fluttering in my stomach, but I actually feel *nauseous*. That must be from the three slices of sweet potato pie I ate last night—I think two must be my limit.

I'm too sick to eat anything, but luckily my ankle feels a whole lot better. Drinking a glass of orange juice, I wonder who helped Mrs. Bosco with all the papers she must have signed for my adoption? If there is one thing I know about the Child Welfare Department, there are more forms to fill out than at the CIA, ABC, or FBI, if you know what I'm sayin'. And normally, I'm the one who helps her fill out forms.

After the kids finish breakfast, I help Mrs. Bosco clear away the plates, then get ready to leave.

"Dorinda, baby, I gotta tell you something," Mrs. Bosco says, walking over to a kitchen chair and sitting down real slow. Pulling out some papers from the knickknack ledge, she coughs, then says slowly, "When I got these papers and signed them, I didn't have my glasses on, so I guess I didn't realize what they were saying."

Mrs. Bosco pauses for a long time, which makes me feel uncomfortable, so I say something to fill up the empty space. "Yeah?"

"Well, Dorinda, I guess the adoption didn't go through," Mrs. Bosco says, letting out a sad sigh. "I found out on Friday, but I didn't want to say anything to your friends, since they were so excited setting up the party and everything,"

I sit there, too stunned to move. "So, I'm not legally adopted or anything?" I ask—but I already know the answer.

"I guess not, baby—but I'm gonna keep trying, you hear," she says, looking at me so sad. "You know how trifling those people downtown can be. They can't do nuttin' right but mess up kids' lives. That's the only thing they seem to do good."

"It doesn't matter," I say, although of course it does. I guess Mrs. Bosco will straighten it out with "those people" eventually. One of these days, I really will get adopted. Still, after all the celebration, it feels pretty empty to know it isn't really true.

I get a sudden urge to ask Mrs. Bosco where my real mother is. Or if it's true she's really around the world on a trip—but I think I already know the answer to that. Besides, looking at how sad Mrs. Bosco is, I don't think it's a good time to talk about it now.

"I don't mind being a foster child," I say, "as long as *you* are my foster mother."

She lets out another sigh. "You always were the smartest child I ever had. Nuttin' you can't do if you put your mind to it. That's what I always said."

At least I can be sure of one thing—if Mrs. Bosco went to all that trouble to adopt me, then no matter what happens, at least I don't have to worry about her giving me away, right?

I decide this is as good a time as any to ask her for the one thing I *really* want. "Can I call you Mom now, instead of Mrs. Bosco?"

"Yes, baby. I guess after all these years we've been together, you can call me anything you want!" Mrs. Bosco beams at me, then pulls out a tissue to cough.

I know it would be pushing too much if I started hugging her, so I don't. And I don't wanna start crying again like a crybaby, as Kenya says, so I tie my jacket around my waist and get up to go. "See ya later, Mom."

"See ya, baby," my foster mom says.

It's a good thing I'm early for rehearsal, because my stomach starts acting up again, and this gives me a chance to sit on the studio floor and calm down.

Pigeon girl from the audition was right. So far, there seem to be exactly five dancers. There are two guys and three girls, including me. They are all definitely older than I am, but they are all kinda small, like me—okay, they're taller, but not *that* much taller.

I smile at the dancer with long black hair down to her waist. She is so pretty. I don't remember seeing her at the audition. She musta been near the front or something.

She smiles back and introduces herself. "Hi, I'm Ling Oh."

"Hi, I'm Dorinda," I say, because I'm not sure if she just told me her first name, or her first and last name—so I wanna be on the safe side. Now I feel sorta self-conscious, because all the dancers are wearing black leotards, and I'm wearing my cheetah all-in-one. It makes me feel like a spotted mistake in the jiggy jungle!

Rubbing my ankle, I hear cackling in the hallway, and a whole group of people comes in, bringing in the noise.

Omigod, I can't believe my eyes. It really is Mo' Money Monique herself!

She is *really* pretty. Her hair is really straight, and her skin is a pretty tan color, and she isn't even wearing any makeup. I read in *Sistarella* magazine that she is sixteen now, but she still lives with her mom in Atlanta.

Mo' Money Monique adjusts her black leotard, and stands next to Dorka, the choreographer.

"Hi, Ms. Dorka," I say, because I can't pronounce her last name, and I don't want to embarrass myself by trying.

"Hello, Dor-een-da. I'm so glad to see you."

Mo' Money Monique comes over and introduces herself to us. We introduce ourselves back, and then she says to me, "I love your leotard, it's dope."

Word, she's *really* nice!

Dorka then takes over, and tells us that we are going to be practicing the moves without music first, just to get the combinations down.

The moves in hip-hop dancing are all about attitude. You have to move quick, sharp, *and* give attitude, as opposed to being graceful, like with jazz. For me, that's what makes it so dope.

Suddenly, it hits me that I'm doing what I've always dreamed of doing—dancing in real life, instead of in the clouds—and yet, I don't feel happy at all. I don't even feel nervous anymore. I just feel, well, *sad*.

At the end of rehearsal, the not-so-jolly giant from the audition, who it turns out is also the principal dancer, tells us to fill out a form.

That's when it hits me. I don't want to fill out any form. I don't want to be a backup dancer. I wanna be like Mo' Money Monique—the star. And if I can't be with my crew, then I don't want to be here, 'cuz I really am a Cheetah Girl.

Now my legs are shaking, as I go over to Dorka to break the news. "I can't do this, Ms. Dorka," I say, even though I'm so nervous, my throat feels like it's shaking.

"You can't do what?" she responds.

"I, um, can't go on the tour—because I'm already in a group," I say, proud of myself that I'm acting like a Cheetah instead of a scaredy cat.

"What kind of group, Dor-een-da?" Dorka asks, genuinely interested in what I have to say.

"We're the Cheetah Girls. It's five of us, and we sing and dance, and we're gonna travel all over the world one day too."

Now Dorka seems amused. "I remember when I left my country to come to America. I got accepted to ballet school here, and I was so scared that I told my mother, 'I don't want to go.' Do-reen-da, I hope you're not doing the same thing, are you?" She gives me a searching look.

"No. I'm not scared anymore. I'm just sad," I reply. "Sad that I could let myself forget so quickly how happy I was that the Cheetah Girls wanted *me* in their group."

"Okay, Dor-een-da. It's up to you. We would like you to tour with us, but remember, there are hundreds of girls who would be very happy to be in your place."

"I know, Ms. Dorka, and I'm sorry, but right now, I'm not one of those girls. I'm a Cheetah Girl."

"Good-bye then—Cheetah Girl," Ms. Dorka says, smiling. "God's gift is a good name for you. You are very brave, and also very talented. And so young, too . . . only twelve years old."

I gasp. How did she know? Of course—Mrs. Bosco must've told her.

"We would have gotten a tutor for you and everything," Dorka says. "Of course, it will be less expensive to hire someone older than you—but you are very special. I'm sure you and your Cheetah Girls will be touring the world someday, just as you say."

"Thanks, Ms. Dorka," I say. "Bye, now. Bye, everyone."

"Good-bye, Dorinda!" they all say, waving to me as I walk out the door, and close it behind me forever.

When I walk outside onto Lafayette Street, I practically run all the way to Chanel's house, which is only a few blocks away. I am so mad at myself for missing rehearsal with my crew! I should have made up my mind yesterday, but I guess I really wanted to know if I got the job for the Mo' Money Monique tour—*for real*, if you know what I'm sayin'.

"Well, looky, looky," says Aqua, when I walk into the exercise studio in Chanel's loft, where my crew have just finished rehearsing.

"We didn't think you were coming," Bubbles says, her eyes twinkling. Her hair looks nice. She's put it up with one of those cheetah squingee hair things.

"I didn't think I was, either, but I missed y'all too much—so I'm not going on that tour," I blurt out. "I'd rather be 'po' up from the floor up,' and a broke Cheetah Girl, than some back-up dancer."

All four of them jump up and down, and start yelling and screaming.

"Chanel, what's going on in there?" Juanita yells from the kitchen.

"*Nada, Mamí!*" Chanel yells back. "We're just happy!"

"We knew you'd be back," Bubbles says, poking out her mouth at me. "Now, listen. We only got a week left before we perform at the Apollo Amateur Hour contest. But we're gonna sing 'Wanna-be Stars in the Jiggy Jungle,' okay? I mean, we rocked the house at the Kats and Kittys Klub Halloween bash with that number, remember?"

"Yeah, that was a dope night," I say. Then I realize something. "Hey, how come you didn't write a song about *me*?"

Bubbles gives me that cheetah-licious look of hers, and says, "Who said I didn't? I just didn't finish it yet."

"What's it called?" I ask, excited.

"Guess."

"Do' Re Mi, Can't You See?"

All four of them heckle me, and Aqua says,

"We'd be po' for sho' if you wuz writing the songs!"

Bubbles stops laughing long enough to say, "The song's called, 'Who's 'Bout to Bounce, Baby?'"

"Word. That's dope."

Juanita walks into the studio, huffing. She's wearing her running sweats and shoes, and she's got a towel around her neck. "Let's hit the road, girls. Running your mouth isn't the same thing as running, *está bien*?"

"What? You mean we're running *again*?" Angie moans.

"That's right," Juanita says sharply. "Any complaints?"

"Dag on," Angie says. "We sure do run a lot."

"Yeah, well, I'm ready for Freddy today, baby," Bubbles says, giving me a little squeeze of affection.

Without any further delay, we hightail it down to the East River and start running uptown. One week until show time, I tell myself as we go. That is really, really dope.

Bubbles is right. We are "ready for Freddy." We're gonna rock the Apollo, so what you know about that, huh?

Who's 'Bout to Bounce?

I look around at my crew—Chanel up front as usual, the rest of us lagging behind—and I realize something. In spite of everything that's gone down, they still don't know the *whole* truth about me.

Telling them I'm really twelve years old right now might push my crew right over the edge. I mean, they put up with me lying to them about the Mo' Money Monique tour, but I'd better not rock the boat again—at least not for a while.

While I'm at it, I decide I'm not going to tell my crew that I'm not legally adopted, either. If I do, then I'll have to tell them what happened, and I don't wanna embarrass my mom.

"My mom . . ." I like the way that sounds. Besides, I know they want me to be happy, so I wanna pretend that I'm adopted for a while longer. Who knows? Maybe by the time I decide to tell them, Mrs. Bosco will have adopted me for real.

Anyway, the deal is, I can be a good friend to my crew, and still keep one or two little secrets to myself, you know what I'm sayin'?

By the time we get to 23rd Street, I notice something very strange. I've been so busy thinking about stuff that I suddenly realize I'm running by myself. Even Angie, Aqua, and Bubbles are running faster than me!

I can't believe that—*Bubbles*, running faster than *me*! She should eat sweet potato pie *every* day! Trying to catch up, I yell, "Hey, Bubbles, wait up!"

She pays me no mind, and yells back, without looking, "Yo, God's gift to the world—*catch up if you can*!" That sends them all into Cheetah heckles.

Yeah, I'm back, all right. Back where I belong. I'm not a wanna-be—not when I'm with my crew. That's what the world needs now and they're gonna get some at the Apollo Theatre, on Saturday night!

Wanna-be Stars in the Jiggy Jungle

Some people walk with a panther
or strike a buffalo stance
that makes you wanna dance.

Other people flip the script
on the day of the jackal
that'll make you cackle.

But peeps like me
got the Cheetah Girl groove
that makes your body move
like wanna-be stars in the jiggy jungle.

The jiggy jiggy jungle!
The jiggy jiggy jungle!

So don't make me bungle
my chance to rise for the prize
and show you who we are
in the jiggy jiggy jungle!
The jiggy jiggy jungle!

Some people move like snakes in the grass
or gorillas in the mist
who wanna get dissed.

Some people dance with the wolves
or trot with the fox
right out of the box.

But peeps like me
got the Cheetah Girl groove
that makes your body move
like wanna-be stars in the jiggy jungle.

The jiggy jiggy jungle!
The jiggy jiggy jungle!

So don't make me bungle
my chance to rise for the prize
and show you who we are
in the jiggy jiggy jungle!
The jiggy jiggy jungle!

Some people lounge with the Lion King
or hunt like a hyena
because they're large and in charge.

Some people hop to it like a hare
because they wanna get snared
or bite like baboons and jump too soon.

But peeps like me
got the Cheetah Girl groove
that makes your body move
like wanna-be stars in the jiggy jungle.

The jiggy jiggy jungle.
The jiggy jiggy jungle.

So don't make me bungle
my chance to rise for the prize
and show you who we are
in the jiggy jiggy jungle!

The jiggy jiggy jungle.
The jiggy jiggy jungle.

Some people float like a butterfly
or sting like a bee
'cuz they wanna be like posse.

Some people act tough like a tiger
to scare away the lynx
but all they do is double jinx.

But peeps like me
got the Cheetah Girl groove
that makes your body move
like wanna-be stars in the jiggy jungle.

The jiggy jiggy jungle.
The jiggy jiggy jungle.

So don't make me bungle
my chance to rise to the prize
and show you who we are
in the jiggy jiggy jungle.

The jiggy jiggy jungle!
The jiggy jiggy jungle!

The Cheetah Girls Glossary

At the end of her rope-a-dope: To run out of moves. When you wanna give up.

Boo-boo: A mistake. A cuddly dog like Toto.

Boomerang toes: Feet that have corns, bunions, or critter-looking toenails.

Bouffant: A puffed-up hairdo.

Bounce: To leave. To jet. To go away and come back another day.

Cellulite: Lumpy fat that looks like cottage cheese and makes grown-up ladies go to beauty parlors and throw duckets out the bucket trying to get rid of it.

Chitlin' circuit: Wack clubs that don't pay singers well.

Diggable planet: A cool place.

Dopiest dope: The coolest of them all.

Easy-breezy tip: When something doesn't take a lot of effort. When you're not sweatin' it.

Knuckleheads: Bozos who don't have jobs and hang out all day doing nothing.

Large and in charge: Successful.

Mad moves: To dance really well.

My face is cracked: I'm embarrassed.

Not having it: When you don't like something.

Penguin feet: Dancer's feet that are slightly pointed outward.

Pigeons: Girls with fake eyeballs and tick-tacky weaves.

Rope-a-dope: When you're doing something *really* well—like double Dutch jump rope, freestyle moves.

She's on a jelly roll: When someone is jammin' with snaps, knowledge, or moves.

Something is jumping off: When something is about to happen.

Stub-a-nubs: Fingernails that have been chomp-a-roni'd to the max.

Whazzup: A popular salutation for greeting members of your crew.

Word: Right. I hear that. Is that right? I know that's right.

PHOTO BY CHARLIE PIZZARELLO

ABOUT THE AUTHOR

Deborah Gregory earned her growl power as a diva-about-town contributing writer for ESSENCE, VIBE, and MORE magazines. She has showed her spots on several talk shows including OPRAH, RICKI LAKE, and MAURY POVICH. She lives in New York City with her pooch, Cappuccino, who is featured as the Cheetah Girls' mascot, Toto.

PHOTO BY TREVOR BROWN

 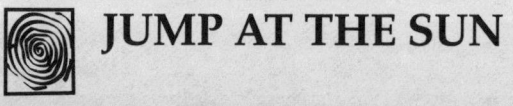 JUMP AT THE SUN

Hey, Girlfriend!

Would you like to be a member of our club?

Just for Me!
by PRO-LINE

VIP CLUB

Join Today!

Become a Just for Me VIP Member and get the official club membership kit today!

The membership kit includes a Just for Me VIP Club: Membership Card, Newsletter, Do Not Disturb Door Hanger, Passport to Fun, Scrungies, Bookmark, Coupons, ID Fingerprint Card, and Membership Flyer. In addition, you will receive a birthday card, a birthday surprise, and bimonthly newsletters.

Official Enrollment Form: Make sure you fill this form out completely. Print clearly. We cannot be responsible for lost, late, misdirected, or illegible mail. Enclose $9.95 plus one Just for Me proof of purchase (front panel), for membership in the JFM VIP Club, or $19.95 with no proof of purchase. Make check or money order (no cash) payable to: Just for Me VIP Club c/o Pro-Line Corp., P.O. Box 222057, Dallas, Texas 75222-9831

Name: _____ Date of Birth: _____

Address: _____

City: _____ State: _____ ZIP: _____

Day Phone: _____ Evening Phone: _____

Parent Signature: _____

Mail membership forms to: Pro-Line Corporation Attn: JFM VIP Club
Membership P.O. Box 222057 Dallas, TX 75222-9831